the inheritance almanac

AN A-TO-Z GUIDE TO THE WORLD OF ERAGON

BY MICHAEL MACAULEY
WITH MARK COTTA VAZ

DOUBLEDAY

www.rbooks.co.uk

THE INHERITANCE ALMANAC
AN A-TO-Z GUIDE TO THE WORLD OF ERAGON
A DOUBLEDAY BOOK 978 0 857 53023 3

First published the United States by Alfred A. Knopf, an imprint of
Random House Children's Books, a division of Random House Inc., New York

Published in Great Britain by Doubleday,
an imprint of Random House Children's Books
A Random House Group Company

This edition published 2010

1 3 5 7 9 10 8 6 4 2

Interior art credits:
© Brom: 34; Fred Gambino, © Random House: 31, 57, 210; Mitchell Gore: 112, 179 (t); © Jupiterimages/Siede Preis:
parchment main text; Michael Macauley: 11; Larry MacDougal, © Random House: 66, 69; Ian Miller, © Random House:
60, 80, 82, 98, 168, 173, 192, 196; © John Jude Palencar: 152; © Christopher Paolini: 7, 14, 87, 125, 191; © Kenneth
Paolini: 24, 25, 61 (r), 147, 166 (l); © Random House: vii, 6, 17, 33, 73, 86, 138, 148, 162, 186, 203; © Shutterstock/
Bitanga87: 77; © Shutterstock/Sascha Burkard: 18; © Shutterstock/Chapelle: 133 (l); © Shutterstock/Paula Cobleigh:
79 (r); © Shutterstock/Shchipkova Elena: 206; © Shutterstock/David Gn: 179 (b); © Shutterstock/Matt Hart: 93; ©
Shutterstock/Nataliya Hora: 10; © Shutterstock/Eric Isselée: 28; © Shutterstock/Jklingebiel: 170, 197; © Shutterstock/
Jeffrey T. Kreulen: 195; © Shutterstock/Jaan-Martin Kuusmann: 61 (l): © Shutterstock/loriklazslo: parchment
introduction; © Shutterstock/S. R. Maglione: 53; © Shutterstock/Mike Norton: 103; © Shutterstock/Randy Miamontez:
157; © Shutterstock/Nebojsa I: 158; © Shutterstock/Mark William Penny: 107; © Shutterstock/pirita: 175; © Shutter-
stock/PZDesigns: 166 (r); © Shutterstock/Pushkin: dragon chapter headings; © Shutterstock/Alexander Ryabintsev: 47;
© Shutterstock/Lori N Skeen: 94; © Shutterstock/Sergio Snitzler: 37; © Shutterstock/Christophe Testi: 133 (c);
© Shutterstock/thoron: 133 (r); © Shutterstock/ultimathule: 127; © Shutterstock/vblinov: 79 (l)

The Random House Group Limited supports The Forest Stewardship Council (FSC),
the leading international forest certification organisation. All our titles that are printed
on Greenpeace approved FSC certified paper carry the FSC logo.
Our paper procurement policy can be found at www.rbooks.co.uk/environment.

Mixed Sources
Product group from well-managed
forests and other controlled sources
FSC   www.fsc.org   Cert no. TT-COC-2139
© 1996 Forest Stewardship Council

RANDOM HOUSE CHILDREN'S BOOKS
61–63 Uxbridge Road, London W5 5SA

www.kidsatrandomhouse.co.uk
www.rbooks.co.uk

Addresses for companies within The Random House Group Limited can be found at:
www.randomhouse.co.uk/offices.htm

THE RANDOM HOUSE GROUP Limited Reg. No. 954009

A CIP catalogue record for this book is available from the British Library.

Printed and bound in Great Britain by Clays Ltd, St Ives plc.

A Word from Michael

Kvetha Fricaya!

In 1998, a young Christopher Paolini sat down in his home in Montana, pen and paper in hand, to embark upon what would become a great and unique adventure: the creation of *Eragon*. A worldwide fantasy phenomenon, the Inheritance cycle has sparked millions of copies in dozens of languages across the globe, a movie adaptation, video games, merchandise, and more. However, the young author's success was far from instant. For the better part of a year, at the age of fifteen, Christopher pored over outlines, notes, and pages of his story, weaving characters and conflict into the tales that we have come to appreciate and enjoy. Shortly after the completion of the first draft of *Eragon*, he chose to show the story to his family. They were immediately captivated by the magic and creativity of the tale and began discussing ways to share his adventure with the world. Confident that Christopher's story would find an audience in Montana and beyond, the family planned to self-publish the book through their small company. Together, the Paolinis spent months editing the manuscript and preparing the book for print before finally launching a promotional tour that would put Christopher in front of crowds of readers looking to get their hands on a new, enthralling tale of action and adventure.

After months of hard work and travel spreading word of the book that they so fervently believed in, a self-published copy of *Eragon* made its way into the hands of editors at Alfred A. Knopf Books for Young Readers. Renowned author Carl Hiaasen recommended the book to his editors at Alfred A. Knopf Books for Young Readers after his stepson purchased and gobbled up a copy during a trip to Montana. Acquisition of publication rights for the entire series—then a proposed trilogy—quickly followed Knopf's initial interest, and the journey of

Christopher Paolini, international bestselling fantasy author, had begun. Over a decade later, the first three books in the Inheritance cycle have permeated cultures and spanned continents.

Christopher Paolini's achievements as a young author in the often-challenging world of publishing have been a continuing source of inspiration to his readers and have shown aspiring young authors that creating works of their own is an entirely accomplishable goal with the right amount of creativity and effort. Inspired by the Paolini family's hands-on approach to self-publishing and marketing, fans and their families began publishing their own books, harnessing the Internet to spread the word. Other fans have chosen alternate routes online, using fan-fiction and story-sharing websites to tell their own tales, whether they take place in the Inheritance universe or in an entirely new world.

"It's overwhelming. I feel as if I am living in an illusion, a dream where all things are possible. Amazing things do happen, I know, but always to someone else, always in some far-off place and time." —Eragon

Like Christopher, I began my journey through the Inheritance world as a fifteen-year-old seeking a creative project to occupy my time over an uneventful winter break. I had recently read *Eragon*, then still a new book on the shelves of our local bookstore, and was fascinated with both the tale he wrote and the story behind it. My interest in websites and fan communities led to my decision to create the first website for Inheritance fans—Shurtugal.com. I worked for weeks to build a centralized storehouse of information on the series, establishing a community for those who wished to join in discussing the books and creating a portal for news on the series' latest developments. Over the next six years, I matured alongside the Inheritance cycle: I traveled around the world to report on the cycle and represent its fans; spent long days and even longer nights scouring the Internet for news; dissected the books for theories; led discussions into In-

Christopher Paolini, international bestselling fantasy author, had begun. Over a decade later, the first three books in the Inheritance cycle have permeated cultures and spanned continents.

Christopher Paolini's achievements as a young author in the often-challenging world of publishing have been a continuing source of inspiration to his readers and have shown aspiring young authors that creating works of their own is an entirely accomplishable goal with the right amount of creativity and effort. Inspired by the Paolini family's hands-on approach to self-publishing and marketing, fans and their families began publishing their own books, harnessing the Internet to spread the word. Other fans have chosen alternate routes online, using fan-fiction and story-sharing websites to tell their own tales, whether they take place in the Inheritance universe or in an entirely new world.

"It's overwhelming. I feel as if I am living in an illusion, a dream where all things are possible. Amazing things do happen, I know, but always to someone else, always in some far-off place and time." —Eragon

Like Christopher, I began my journey through the Inheritance world as a fifteen-year-old seeking a creative project to occupy my time over an uneventful winter break. I had recently read *Eragon*, then still a new book on the shelves of our local bookstore, and was fascinated with both the tale he wrote and the story behind it. My interest in websites and fan communities led to my decision to create the first website for Inheritance fans—Shurtugal.com. I worked for weeks to build a centralized storehouse of information on the series, establishing a community for those who wished to join in discussing the books and creating a portal for news on the series' latest developments. Over the next six years, I matured alongside the Inheritance cycle: I traveled around the world to report on the cycle and represent its fans; spent long days and even longer nights scouring the Internet for news; dissected the books for theories; led discussions into Inheritance's past, present, and future; and most importantly, had the opportunity to work closely with the people who made the entire series possible. My work at the heart of the Inheritance community over the past decade has given me a perspective that few fans have had the chance to experience. Recognizing this as an adventure that all readers would want to share in, I set out to use my knowledge and resources to create an almanac that would entertain, inform, and excite fans. The result of my experiences, efforts, and love for the world of Alagaësia is *The Inheritance Almanac,* a comprehensive look at both the important and overlooked characters, landmarks, events, and conflicts of the Inheritance cycle.

> *"Oaths betrayed, souls killed, eggs shattered! Blood everywhere. Murderers!"*
> —Saphira

The Inheritance cycle is a fusion of action and adventure, love and loathing, victory and defeat; it is a journey through the trials and triumphs of Eragon Shadeslayer and his companion, Saphira Brightscales, who together comprise the last free dragon and Rider of Alagaësia. The pair set out to rid their beloved continent of the evil unleashed upon the world after Galbatorix claimed the throne. During their journey, they experience wonders that baffle the mind: mountains greater than our world's tallest skyscrapers; monsters thought to dwell only in the dark chasms of nightmares; majestic races of mystery and legend; and conflicts that threaten to rip apart the very fabric of the world. Their discoveries and experiences, allies and enemies, are chronicled in thousands of exquisitely detailed pages. It was clear that collecting and organizing this information to prevent losing it to the dustbins of history would be a task that at one time would have been undertaken by no one but the most devoted monks of Arcaena.

> *"What wisdom can I give people that they haven't already learned? What feats*

can I achieve that an army couldn't do better? It's insanity!"   —Eragon

The Inheritance Almanac is a compendium of knowledge and information, from the known to the unknown, the serious to the absurd, detailing the expansive history of Alagaësia. This tome enables Inheritance adventurers to refresh their memories while exploring such topics as Murtagh and the battalions of soldiers who cannot feel pain. Readers will uncover the mysteries of the Eldunarí, the heavily guarded secret of the dragon race; journey through the ruins of Edur Ithindra, one of Alagaësia's most ancient elf outposts; conquer the treacherous Spine mountain range; and roam the harsh and unforgiving Hadarac Desert. The *Almanac* will answer many readers' questions, rekindle distant memories, and inspire new ways of interpreting the cycle's contents.

Fantasy sleuths and Inheritance fanatics will immediately recognize Christopher's homages to fantasy and science-fiction works that have inspired and entertained him scattered throughout the *Almanac*. These hidden gems have provided dedicated fans with a "mini-game" of hunting down Christopher's latest references, from the obvious, such as the dwarf king Hrothgar, a direct allusion to Hrothgar, ruler of Denmark in the Anglo-Saxon epic *Beowolf*, to trickier references, including the "lonely god," a modern-day reference to the British science-fiction television show *Doctor Who*. And there are real-world character and location inspirations, such as Christopher's sister, Angela, whose personality provided the basis for Angela the herbalist, and his home amid the picturesque Montana landscape, which inspired much of Palancar Valley's beauty.

Whether you are a fan of many years or a new reader just beginning your journey through the Inheritance cycle, the *Almanac* will serve as a trusty companion while you experience Alagaësia in its full measure of glory. So brace yourself, for turning the page will begin an epic adventure through a collection of knowledge and information on par with the renowned historical volumes of the Arcaena monks. You are about to delve into Alagaësia's most elusive depths.

Atra esterní ono thelduin,
Mor'ranr lífa unin hjarta onr,
Un du evarínya ono varda.

"And now for the greatest adventure of all."　　　　　　　　　　— Brom

Michael Macauley
October 2010

CHRISTOPHER PAOLINI (LEFT) AND MICHAEL MACAULEY

Aberon

In southern Alagaësia, in the pastoral countryside, stands Aberon, the walled capital city of Surda, the free nation of human beings. The heart of Aberon is Borromeo Castle, where King Orrin and the royal family live and rule in defiance of King Galbatorix and the Empire. Orrin's government has played a key role in the uprising, forging a working alliance with the Varden (the major resistance group to the Empire) and providing sanctuary for refugees and opposition leaders.

Borromeo Castle is an austere edifice reflecting the spartan reality of wartime and has heartened Orrin's countrymen, as it embodies the government's serious focus in this time of crisis. The exigency of wartime can be seen in Borromeo's fortifications: three rings of stone walls, with numerous lookout towers atop each, and hundreds of ballistae ready to unleash offensive firepower. Orrin's one indulgence is the laboratory he maintains within the castle walls, where he pursues his scientific interests.

Acallamh

The name of one of two lovers from the song "Du Silbena Datia." The other is Nuada.

Aethrid

The woman celebrated in the song "Sweet Aethrid o' Dauth."
See Edel.

After Creation (AC)

According to the dwarven calendar, "After Creation" (AC) marks recorded history from when the god Helzvog formed the first dwarves. Major historic events based on this calendar include

> 5217 AC: The date elves are believed to have landed in Alagaësia near the site of present-day Teirm.
>
> 5291–5296 AC: The seminal struggle between dragons and elves. This conflict is referred to as Du Fyrn Skulblaka in the ancient language (the Dragon War).
>
> 5296 AC: The Dragon Riders are born of the peace pact between dragons and elves.
>
> 5596 AC: The first humans, known as the Broddrings, appear on the Surdan coast. After trading with dwarves, they disappear back whence they came. Human beings return in 7203 AC and establish permanent settlements.
>
> 7206 AC: Dragon Riders widen the pact between dragons and elves to include human Riders.
>
> 7886 AC: The Dragon Rider Galbatorix begins his bloody rise to power in Alagaësia.

7896–7900 AC: The period known as the Fall of the Dragon Riders, which culminates in the death of Rider leader Vrael and victory over the Broddring nation, whereupon Galbatorix declares himself king.

7900–7903 AC: The Varden, a rebel alliance, is founded by humans to fight Galbatorix's Empire while other humans form the independent state of Surda.

7903 AC: The year in which Jeod Longshanks and Brom, last of the Dragon Riders, rescue a dragon egg from Galbatorix. The egg subsequently hatches into Saphira, the dragon raised by Eragon, a fifteen-year-old human dwelling in the village of Carvahall in Palancar Valley.

AGAETÍ BLÖDHREN

This elven festivity, whose name means "Blood-oath Celebration," is held once every century to honor the sacred pact that ended the war between dragons and elves and formed the Dragon Riders. Held around the Menoa tree in the heart of the Du Weldenvarden forest, this joyous three-day festival is marked by music, dancing, and feasting. A highlight of the celebration is a renewal of the bond between dragons and Riders. It is performed by the Caretakers, two ancient elves who wield the combined power of every dragon in Alagaësia and can bestow this energy upon a chosen one—most recently, Eragon.

The elven Dragon Rider Oromis warned Eragon to be on his guard during the Agaetí Blödhren, explaining that even elves can go mad—"wonderfully, gloriously mad, but mad all the same." Eragon and Saphira indeed found themselves drawn into what Oromis called "the web of our magic." The celebration passed like a dream, with Eragon lulled by songs and dancing, strange sights of animals drawn out of the woods, and elves perched on the Menoa tree, which seemed to sway to the energy pulsating around it.

It is a tradition that everyone share a poem, song, or piece of art at the Agaetí Blödhren. On the third day, Eragon and Saphira each did so. Eragon had prepared verse that Queen Islanzadí proclaimed helped them all understand his difficult journey as a Dragon Rider, a work of such distinction she would add it to her great library in Tialdarí Hall. Saphira offered artwork to the elves, a large black stone sculpture bathed in fire that made the rock appear alive.

The ceremony concluded with the Caretakers, Iduna and Nëya, both clad only in their iridescent dragon tattoos, magically conjuring a dragon that touched Eragon's gedwëy ignasia (a distinctive mark on a Dragon Rider's palm). Overnight, Eragon experienced the physical transformation a human Rider undergoes over time. Eragon not only came to physically resemble an elf, but he later realized the supernatural dragon had also imparted to him elvish strength and speed.

SEE CARETAKERS AND GEDWËY IGNASIA.

AGE OF HERRAN

In the history of the dwarf nation, the period during which the great dwarf sculptor Dûrok Ornthrond carved the gigantic gem known as Isidar Mithrim.

AJIHAD

A leader of the Varden, the rebel alliance fighting Galbatorix's Empire. Ajihad and his daughter, Nasuada, joined the Varden shortly after the rebellion was founded. Little is known of their past, although it is believed that father and daughter lived among the nomads of the Hadarac Desert before joining the Varden. From the beginning, Ajihad worked tirelessly for the cause and swiftly rose in influence and power. When the Varden leader Deynor died, Ajihad became the new leader.

The Urgals, then the enemies of the Varden, honored him with the name

Nightstalker, a term of respect, "because of how he hunted [them] in the dark tunnels under the dwarf mountain and because of the color of his hide." Ajihad fought in many battles against the Empire. Ajihad also welcomed Eragon and Saphira to the Varden sanctuary in Farthen Dûr, telling the young Dragon Rider the Varden were hoping for the best from him, but also giving a warning: "Everyone knows what the Varden want—or the Urgals, or even Galbatorix—but no one knows what you want. And that makes you dangerous, especially to Galbatorix. He fears you because he doesn't know what you will do next."

Ajihad showed his mettle as he led his forces against an Urgal army fighting for Galbatorix that had invaded the Varden sanctuary, the great struggle known as the Battle of Farthen Dûr. The Varden won, but even when that fight was over, Ajihad spent three days hunting the remnants of the Urgal army through the ancient tunnels the dwarves had built under Farthen Dûr and throughout the Beor Mountains. Ajihad was among ten men who were returning to the dwarven capital of Tronjheim when a pack of Urgals attacked. Ajihad fought fiercely, killing five Urgals, but fell, mortally wounded. Eragon and the elven princess Arya witnessed this. As Eragon approached and knelt by his commander, he saw the Varden leader's breastplate hacked open, heard his labored breathing. Ajihad, with his dying breath, asked Eragon to promise not to let the Varden fall into chaos. They were the only hope for resisting Galbatorix, Ajihad said, and had to be kept strong.

Ajihad had ruled for fifteen years. At a meeting to decide the transfer of power, Varden commander Jörmundur recalled that Ajihad had done more than anyone to oppose the Empire, that he had led and won "countless battles against superior forces," that he had nearly killed Durza, a Shade, and had welcomed the Dragon Rider Eragon and his dragon, Saphira, into the Varden sanctuary. But "a new leader must be chosen, one who will win us even more glory," Jörmundur declared. The slain leader's own daughter, Nasuada, was ultimately entrusted with that solemn duty.

See AJIHAD'S TOMB.

Ajihad's tomb

In honor of all he had done for the free races of Alagaësia, Ajihad was buried within the great chamber under Farthen Dûr where dwarves are entombed. During the funeral procession, Ajihad's body was lain on a white marble bier and carried by six men dressed in armor the color of mourning black. A helm of precious stones was upon Ajihad's head, and he was laid to rest with his mighty sword and shield.

Although Ajihad, being human, could not be buried with dwarves, a special alcove was prepared where the Varden and others could come to pay their respects without disturbing the sacred spaces dedicated to the dwarves. His burial place was past a graveyard of glistening crystal, down into a catacomb of alcoves lit by red lanterns. Above his crypt, this tribute was carved in dwarven runes:

May all, Knurlan, Humans, and Elves,
Remember
This Man.
For he was Noble, Strong, and Wise.
Gûntera Arûna

See dwarven burial rites.

Alagaësia

The continent of Alagaësia is home to dragons, dwarves, elves, humans, Urgals, and the nomadic tribes and artisans descended from the wandering tribes. Some races have migrated from the legendary land of Alalëa, as the elves call this mysterious place of their origins. In addition to the Empire of Galbatorix, which is basically the former cities and territory of the Broddring nation, there is the independent human state of Surda in the southwest.

Geographic features include the western coastal mountain range of the

Spine, which includes numerous human settlements; the forest of Du Welden-varden to the north, the largest forest on the continent and home to the elven people; the Hadarac Desert, which spreads across much of the land and has tradi-tionally been home to wild dragons; and the Beor Mountains to the south, where the dwarves make their home.

Magic is woven into the land and has even been used to transform the natural world, as the elves have done in the cities they have formed out of the trees and other plant life of Du Weldenvarden.

SEE ANCIENT LANGUAGE.

CHRISTOPHER PAOLINI'S MAP OF ALAGAËSIA,
WHICH HE DREW WHEN HE WAS WRITING *ERAGON*.

Alalëa

This legendary second continent of the world is shrouded in mystery—even the elves who migrated from this place have not revealed anything about the land of their origins. Much of this mystery is due to the great unknown of what lies across the seas and beyond the horizon. The ancient language word for Alalëa is reserved for only the rarest and most important occasions and roughly translates as "a melancholy dream of great beauty."

Alanna

See elf children.

Alarice, Lady

See Dauth.

Albatross

A Nardan ship.

Albriech

One of Horst and Elain's two sons. Albriech and his brother, Baldor, gave valuable help to Roran when the Empire invaded Carvahall and during the villagers' flight to join the Varden. The burly sons also help their father in blacksmithing for the Varden.

ALDEN

SEE SLOAN.

ALDHRIM

Dwarf chief of Dûrgrimst Ingeitum prior to the leadership of Hrothgar, the future dwarf king.

SEE DWARF CLANS *IN THE APPENDIX.*

AMA

One of the guards for the dwarf clan chief Ûndin.

ANALÍSIA

The great elf bard. One of Analísia's epics was read by Eragon during his stay in Ellesméra, capital city of the elves.

ANCIENT LANGUAGE

An enduring remnant of Alagaësia's ancient history is the original language of truth and magic created by the indigenous race known as the Grey Folk. Although lost for a time, the ancient language was reintroduced by the elves, a people of innate magical qualities. Because the ancient language is bound to the energy of the world, to speak it is to harness great power. Elven celebrations where songs are sung in the ancient language create bewitching spells that can be intoxicating to elves but dangerous to humans and other outsiders.

Among its attributes, the ancient language describes the true nature of things, and one cannot directly lie while speaking it. Masters of the ancient language can cast spells and make others do what they want. Although Dragon Riders were traditionally trained in the magical language, even they had to use it correctly, for a mistake could result in unintended consequences, including death. The script itself is composed of forty-two different glyphs, representing different sounds that can be combined in limitless ways to form words and phrases.

See LIDUEN KVAEDHÍ *and* MAGIC.

NEARLY HALF OF *BRISINGR* WAS WRITTEN
WITH AN INK-DIP PEN.

ANGELA THE HERBALIST

In a time when even the most trusted are subjected to intense scrutiny, it is considered a great accomplishment to keep one's past a secret—such an inscrutable figure is Angela the herbalist, a human witch and warrior with a penchant for speaking in riddles and answering questions with questions. In a rare personal revelation, Angela once acknowledged an apprenticeship with the hermit-wizard Tenga, a time she recalled as "unfortunate." It is said she is one of the rare outsiders to have traveled among the elves of Du Weldenvarden before the Fall of the Riders.

What is known about Angela for certain is that she owned the herb and potion shop in the wealthy residential section of the city of Teirm and is often accompanied by Solembum, a shape-shifting werecat. Despite the pair's close companionship, the witch is loathed by the king of the werecat race. Angela has curly brown hair and youthful features but is much older than she looks. Her youthful appearance and radiant health are the result of her herbs and potions. She can read one's future, but usually only those Solembum deems worthy—only five are known to have been so favored, including Eragon and his mother, Selena.

Angela became a freedom fighter when she took up residence among the Varden in their sanctuary of Farthen Dûr, and she proved her valor during the Battle of Farthen Dûr. During the Battle of the Burning Plains, she snuck behind enemy lines to poison the Empire's soldiers. In addition to her fighting ability, her talent as a healer has aided many wounded Varden. Angela is currently an advisor to Nasuada, the Varden leader, and caretaker of Elva.

THE CHARACTER ANGELA IS BASED ON, AND NAMED AFTER, PAOLINI'S SISTER.

ANGELA'S THEORIZING ABOUT THE EXISTENCE OF TOADS AND FROGS IN *ERAGON* IS BASED ON A REAL INCIDENT WITH PAOLINI'S SISTER.

Angela's herbal shop

In Teirm, next to the mansion of Jeod Longshanks, is the shop where Angela and her werecat companion, Solembum, once lived and worked, a rustic structure overrun with tangled vines and leaves where a green-tinted light was usually visible from the obscured windows. Angela closed the shop when she made the decision to follow Eragon to the Varden.

Angrenost, King

See Broddring Kingdom *and* Ilirea.

Angvard

The dwarves' personification of Death, also known as the Gray Man.

Anhûin

The Grimstcarvlorss of a dwarf clan that was once among the oldest and richest in the dwarf nation, Anhûin volunteered to help Vrael, the leader of the Dragon Riders, fight Galbatorix and his Thirteen Forsworn. It was a disaster—all the clan was slaughtered, except for Anhûin and her guards. The grief-stricken keeper of the clan house died soon after, and the survivors adopted a new clan name—Az Sweldn rak Anhûin, meaning "the Tears of Anhûin." The clan bitterly blamed all Dragon Riders and recently declared themselves sworn blood enemies of Eragon and his dragon. It was while Eragon was visiting the dwarven surface city of Tarnag that a strange dwarf made the clan intentions clear by plucking three hairs from his beard, wrapping them around an iron ring, and disdainfully tossing it in the street and spitting. The bitterness was so extreme that the clan actually violated the Law of Hospitality in an attempt to kill the young Dragon Rider.

See Tarnag and Vermûnd.

Anurin

The leader of the Dragon Riders who made the controversial decision to include humans in the magical bond that had exclusively existed between elves and dragons.

See Broddring Kingdom.

Arcaena

The secretive religious sect that originated in the secluded coastal town of Kuasta and is dedicated to collecting and preserving Alagaësia's history and knowledge against the coming of an unspecified catastrophe. The Arcaena core belief can be summed up as follows: "All knowledge is sacred."

Heslant the Monk is one of Arcaena's most renowned keepers of knowledge. His major scholarly work, *Domia Abr Wyrda* (translated as "Dominance of Fate"), is considered the most complete history of the continent. This book's publication angered Galbatorix, who ordered Heslant's execution and the destruction of all copies of his masterpiece.

Aren

Few honors in the world are more prized than this ring, a gift from the leader of the elves. The ring Aren, carved by the greatest elven artisans, is designed as a golden band set with a rare and powerful sapphire upon which is etched the yawë, a mystic elven symbol. The ring can store massive amounts of energy, but its true significance is that it marks its wearer as a friend and ally of the elves.

Aren was personally bestowed by elf queen Islanzadí upon the great Dragon Rider Brom. After Brom's death at the hands of the monstrous Ra'zac, Eragon came into possession of the ring. Brom had been storing energy within it for years, and it had accumulated great power by the time Eragon took possession. His ownership of the ring was made official during his first encounter with Queen Islanzadí, forever marking Eragon as a revered friend of the elves.

 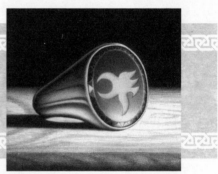

CHRISTOPHER PAOLINI'S
ILLUSTRATION OF AREN.

ARGETLAM

An elven word used to refer to a Dragon Rider. It literally means "silver hand," referring to the gedwëy ignasia ("shining palm") that all Riders bear.

ARGHEN

In dwarven legend, a dwarf who sleeps forever in a cave.

AROUGHS

This isolated city on the southwestern border of Alagaësia is firmly in the Empire's control, but its isolation makes it vulnerable to attack. After one Varden attack, Galbatorix ordered the bolstering of Aroughs's defenses. North of the city gates are the bogs where the phenomenon of werelights can be seen.

ARVA

A loyal servant of the Dragon Riders of Vroengard during the time of their downfall at the hands of Galbatorix's forces. During Galbatorix's Siege of Ilirea (Urû'baen), Arva was among those desperately fighting to save the city. Despite Arva's valor, he fell at the hands of Kialandí, a member of the Thirteen Forsworn. Before his death, Arva gave his sister, Naudra, his Rider sword, Támerlein. She fought valiantly at his side during his final day. When all was lost, Naudra, though gravely injured, fought free of the invaders and fled the city, only later to succumb to her wounds.

ARVINDR

One of the Dragon Rider swords.

ARYA

The daughter of King Evander and Queen Islanzadí and an ambassador of the elf nation. For nearly a century, Arya Dröttningu ("Princess Arya" in the ancient language) has served as ambassador to the allied nations. Recently, Arya's key role was as protector and courier of the dragon egg in the possession of the elves and the Varden.

From her earliest years growing up in the capital city of Ellesméra, much was expected of Arya. The young royal not only exceeded the expectations of her family but also quelled the reservations of her critics, becoming superior in spell-casting and swordsmanship. The one distraction of her youth was a young male elf named Fäolin. The two were virtually inseparable, but their relationship was not destined to blossom.

Soon after the death of her father, Arya volunteered to be guardian of the dragon egg that had been taken from Galbatorix, ferrying it back and forth between the elves and the Varden, hoping it would hatch for someone. The queen opposed this appointment, rightly fearing for her daughter's safety. But Arya, with steely determination, was made royal guardian of the egg and ambassador to the Varden, with Fäolin joining the royal guard to be near her. This appointment led to an estrangement from her mother that lasted seventy years.

Queen Islanzadí's worst fears were realized when the royal guard was returning from Tronjheim to the elven city of Osilon. The Shade Durza and his Urgal assassins sprang an ambush. Arya's companions, Glenwing and her beloved Fäolin, were slain. Arya was captured, although she managed to magically transport the egg to the Spine, where it was found by Eragon. Arya paid a terrible price, languishing in a prison cell deep within Durza's fortress in Gil'ead, where Durza tortured her in an effort to learn the whereabouts of the egg, the location of the rebel Varden, and other vital concerns of the Empire. She revealed nothing, even when tortured to the edge of death. Her ordeal ended with her rescue by Eragon, the budding young Rider who had seen Arya in his dreams. Eragon himself had been imprisoned in Gil'ead and, with the help of his comrade Murtagh and Saphira (the dragon hatched from the very egg Arya had sworn to protect), Eragon escaped with Arya. The elven princess was taken to the Varden, who nursed her back to health.

Arya resumed her role as ambassador of the elves and fought alongside Eragon and Saphira at the Battle of Farthen Dûr, playing a pivotal role in the Varden victory. However, while riding Saphira, and in an attempt to distract Durza from slaying Eragon, she smashed Isidar Mithrim, the gigantic sculpted gem that was the beloved symbol of the dwarf nation.

Since returning to her homeland, Arya has received the blessings of Queen Islanzadí. She also serves with the elven spellcasters assigned to protect Eragon and Saphira. Eragon, always attracted to the lovely elf, finally professed his love after the Agaetí Blödhren. Arya replied that they were friends and could be nothing more. Her rejection brought Eragon to tears, but she simply told him, "You and I are not meant for each other."

Arya's recent accomplishments include eradicating a second Shade at the Battle of Feinster, an act that made her a Shadeslayer, one of a very select group.

THE REFERENCE ARYA MAKES IN *BRISINGR* TO A "LONELY GOD" WHILE SHE IS SKETCHING GLYPHS ON THE GROUND IS AN ALLUSION TO THE LONG-RUNNING BRITISH TELEVISION PROGRAM *DR. WHO*.

ASCÛDGAMLN

Ascûdgamln, Dwarvish for "fists of steel," is a unique method for making a dwarf's own hands a weapon. In the process, a healer lulls the warrior into a deep sleep, holes are drilled into the knuckles, and a metal socket is embedded and sealed by magic that allows for spikes to be threaded into the sockets. Although the Ascûdgamln are great for hand-to-hand fighting, few dwarves undergo the operation—if a drill goes too deep, the warrior can lose a hand. Ascûdgamln are also not suitable for humans and elves, as dwarves have thicker bones that can withstand the procedure. Eragon, an admirer of this special weapon, created thick calluses resembling Ascûdgamln on his own hands.

ÄTHALVARD

The elven organization devoted to the preservation of elven songs and poems.

AZ KNURLDRÂTHN

Deep within the Beor Mountains, on Mount Thardûr, is this stone formation, estimated to be more than a thousand years old. Az Knurldrâthn ("Trees of Stone") is a mystery—some say it was a granite excavation, others that it was the remnant of an ancient catastrophe, and still others that Helzvog, dwarven god of stone, created it. In recent times, Az Knurldrâthn has become a place of punishment, where wayward dwarven youths are sent to reflect on their wrongdoings.

AZ SINDRIZNARRVEL

Also known as the Gem of Sindri, this enormous replica of the dwarves' flameless lantern was discovered atop a bell tower at the peak of the five-story edifice that makes up Bregan Hold. The teardrop-shaped lantern, used by dwarves in times of emergency and celebration, is held in place by slabs of granite and emits a bright light in hues of gold.

THE FOREST OF STONE IS BASED ON A REAL PETRIFIED FOREST.

AZ SWELDN RAK ANHÛIN

SEE ANHÛIN. SEE ALSO DWARF CLANS IN THE APPENDIX.

Baldor

One of the two sons of Horst and Elain, who took in young Eragon after the death of Eragon's uncle, Garrow. Baldor and his brother, Albriech, also worked closely with Eragon's brother, Roran, who led refugees from Carvahall after the Empire's siege and destruction of their village.

CHRISTOPHER NAMED BALDOR AFTER HIS UNCLE BRUCE.

Banishing of the Names

See Du Namar Aurboda *and* Forsworn.

Barden

This spellcaster of the human nation of Surda rode with King Orrin during the Battle of the Burning Plains to protect him from the Empire's spellcasters.

Battle of Farthen Dûr

The pivotal struggle in which the Varden refuge in Farthen Dûr was penetrated by the Urgal army led by the Shade Durza. It marked Eragon and Saphira's first major battle as Rider and dragon. They fought alongside the elf princess Arya and Murtagh. Murtagh had been viewed with suspicion when he first arrived at the Varden sanctuary with Eragon, but the young swordsman silenced his doubters as he fought valiantly against the invaders.

The battle was won by the Varden. Eragon also fought Durza, killing the Shade with a sword thrust through the heart. Durza's death freed the Urgals, who had been spellbound by Durza's sorcery, and earned Eragon the rare title of Shadeslayer. In the aftermath of the battle, while searching the labyrinthine tunnels under Farthen Dûr for Urgals, the Varden leader Ajihad was killed by them.

Battle of the Burning Plains

The Burning Plains was the site of a major battle between the Varden and the Empire. Each army faced the other across the no-man's-land of a desolate burning plain and the Jiet River's chalky waters. To the south were the tents of the coalition forces of the Varden, which included the men of Surda and King Orrin's cavalry. To the north waited Galbatorix's army, which stretched across three miles and was estimated at upward of a hundred thousand soldiers. Eragon went to battle with Saphira, his sword, Zar'roc, hanging off the belt of Beloth the Wise. At Nasuada's request, Eragon led Du Vrangr Gata, the Varden spellcasters under the command of the sorceress Trianna.

Before the battle, Nar Garzhvog, leader of the Urgals' Bolvek tribe, appeared before Nasuada to admit that his race had once made a deal with Galbatorix in return for land and had become spellbound by the magic of Durza. Now, betrayed by Galbatorix and freed from Durza's enchantment, they wanted to become allies of the Varden to seek their revenge on Galbatorix. The people of Alagaësia had long feared and despised the war-loving Urgals. Ignoring the jeers, fears, and hate of those Varden soldiers for whom the Urgals had long been enemies, Nasuada bravely allowed Garzhvog and his warriors to bivouac along the eastern flank of her army and ultimately join forces with her.

At dawn, the armies clashed. Soldiers attacked with swords, spears, hammers, and pikes; Eragon and the spellcasters of Du Vrangr Gata met their Empire counterparts; and the Empire brought up catapults, trebuchets, ballistae, and other machines of war. That day even the unlikely pair of Garzhvog and Orik, the future dwarf king, gloried in the carnage as they fought side by side. A great push by the Varden, led by dwarven soldiers, beat back, then routed, the Empire. In the ensuing chaos, the confused and panicky soldiers of the Empire lost heart, and those who weren't dying began surrendering or retreating.

Although the Empire was defeated, Eragon and Saphira then witnessed an ominous sight—a Rider and dragon arising from the Empire's side of the battlefield to the pounding of war drums. Eragon realized the sight of a red dragon meant that Galbatorix had gotten one of the two dragon eggs in his possession to hatch. But worse revelations awaited as he discovered the identity of the Rider, whose face had been shielded by a helm—it was his former friend and ally Murtagh, who had been presumed dead after the Battle of Farthen Dûr. Murtagh killed King Hrothgar and captured Eragon. He chose to release Eragon, but before he did so, he took Zar'roc from Eragon and told him that the two of them were brothers—that Murtagh was the eldest son of Morzan and Selena, Eragon the younger. Murtagh thus claimed Zar'roc as his rightful inheritance. Murtagh's revelation was incorrect, but Eragon did not know that then.

SEE BURNING PLAINS, DRAGON RIDER SWORDS, MORZAN, AND MURTAGH.

BATTLE-STORM

The stallion of the Varden leader Nasuada.

BEIRLAND

The largest of five islands off the southwestern coast of Alagaësia and the only inhabited one, with one coastal village, Eoam.

SEE SOUTHERN ISLES.

BELATONA

Home to many of Alagaësia's finest craftsmen, Belatona lies within Empire territory at the juncture of Leona Lake and the Jiet River. Its proximity to the border of Surda and its access to Dras-Leona and beyond has made the city a strategic target of the Varden army. To strengthen Belatona's defenses, Galbatorix garrisoned armed forces within the city.

BELLAEN DU HLJÖDHR

A resident of Ellesméra, whose name means "Bellaen the Silent." When Eragon and his dragon, Saphira, spent time studying and training in Ellesméra, Bellaen was in charge of their needs and comfort. Ballaen also granted Saphira permission to hunt within Du Weldenvarden, provided that her kills were outside elven settlements.

Beloth the Wise/Belt of Beloth the Wise

Little is known of the fabled Dragon Rider Beloth the Wise, although it is said his life's story can be found within accounts of the Year of Darkness. What is known is that he owned the gem-studded sword that bears his name and that was given to Eragon Shadeslayer by Oromis. The woven belt has a pattern of a Lianí Vine; pulling a tassel at the end reveals twelve perfectly cut, multicolored diamonds (white, black, red, blue, yellow, brown) capable of storing a large supply of energy, which the bearer can draw upon when needed.

Beor

See Urzhad.

Beor Mountains

The true name of this mountain range, the largest in Alagaësia, is a closely guarded secret of the dwarves. Its popular name is derived from the ancient language word for the cave bears native to these mountains. The Beor Mountains were populated by the dwarves only after their original home in a verdant land became arid and hot, climate change creating what is today known as the Hadarac Desert. Over time, the dwarves spread throughout the range, establishing both surface and subterranean cities. Today the Beors are home to all but one of the dwarven cities, including the zenith of dwarven architecture and engineering, the capital city of Tronjheim, which is built within the immense volcanic hollow of Farthen Dûr.

The host of animal species unique to the Beor Mountains includes the Fanghur, Feldûnost, Nagra, Shrrg, and Urzhad (the Dwarvish word for the Beor). The mountains reach a peak of ten miles, and access is limited to a valley entryway or the Az Ragni river. Landmarks include Mani's Caves, said to be home of the legendary dream well, and Moldûn the Proud, the northernmost peak of the range.

THE BEOR MOUNTAINS ARE BASED ON THE BEARTOOTH MOUNTAINS IN MONTANA, WHERE CHRISTOPHER PAOLINI LIVES. THE TITANIC SIZE OF THE BEOR MOUNTAINS IS BASED ON THE MOUNTAINS OF NEW ZEALAND, WHICH PAOLINI ONCE HEARD ARE RISING SO FAST, THEY WOULD BE TEN MILES HIGH IF EROSION WASN'T A FACTOR.

BERUNDAŁ

The "ill-marked" subject of an elven song.

BID'DAUM

See Du Fyrn Skulblaka *and* Eragon.

The name Bid'Daum (the first dragon to be paired with a Rider) spelled backward yields Muad'Dib, the main character from the novel *Dune*.

BIRGIT

Wife to Quimby and mother of several children. A resident of the village of Carvahall, Quimby, Carvahall's most skilled brewer, was killed when he intervened in an argument between two drunken Empire soldiers. The tragedy galvanized Birgit into fighting to defend her home and family. She became a warrior, with a natural instinct for extracting herself and others from dangerous situations. During the Empire's siege of Carvahall, Birgit joined the villagers who fled their homes. Birgit blames Roran, Eragon's cousin and leader of Carvahall's refugees, for bringing the Empire's wrath upon them and has sworn to take revenge against him someday. In the meantime, however, she is working with Roran to save the people of Carvahall. When she needs an alias, Birgit assumes her late mother's name, Mardra.

Birgit is often accompanied on journeys by her teenage son, Nolfavrell, who watches over his younger siblings. Nolfavrell proved himself when he killed an Empire soldier during the attack on Carvahall. Like his mother, he desires revenge for his father's death, though he does not hold a grudge against Roran. When he needs an alias, Nolfavrell uses the name Kell.

BIRKA

One of the horses that belong to Garrow of Carvahall.

BJARTSKULAR

The ancient language title for Eragon's dragon, Saphira; it translates as "Brightscales."

BLACK HAND

Galbatorix's elite group of spies, assassins, and spellcasters charged with eliminating key figures in the Varden and within Surda. This secret society was discovered when Drail, trained "in the dark uses of magic," was captured shortly after his attempted assassination of Nasuada, the Varden leader. Before he committed suicide by magic, Drail's mind was searched, providing the Varden with their first knowledge of the Black Hand. The information helped the Varden hunt down, capture, and kill a large portion of its members. But the Black Hand threat remains, and prominent members of the Varden and Surdans are well versed in defending themselves against the Empire's magic attacks and telepathic probes. The Black Hand is Galbatorix's attempt to emulate the role Selena, who herself was known as the Black Hand of Morzan, played for Morzan.

SEE SELENA.

BLACKMOOR SHIPPING COMPANY

This shipping company in Teirm serves as a front for transporting supplies for the Empire's armies.

SEE DRAGON WING.

BLADESINGER

The older of the two females who crossed paths with Eragon, Saphira, and Angela in one of the Varden's war camps in Surda. Bladesinger speaks with an unknown accent; the strips of leather she wears over scarred wrists mark her as having been a slave or a prisoner. Bladesinger is one of the select few to have had her future foretold by Angela the herbalist, who let slip that Bladesinger will have a role in shaping Alagaësia's future. Before her departure from the Varden camp, Eragon offered Bladesinger a blessing in the ancient language. Saphira called Bladesinger "Wolf-Eyes."

Bladesinger's traveling companion was a muscular teenage girl with no name, herself a mysterious figure but deemed important enough for Angela to have cast the dragon knucklebones to divine her future. The girl was also blessed by Eragon when she left the Varden in Bladesinger's company. These are the first blessings Eragon gave since the ill-fated one he bestowed upon Elva.

BLAGDEN

The mysterious raven that saved the life of elf king Evandar during his battle with Urgals. The king rewarded the raven with a magical blessing that increased the bird's intelligence and extended its life span. However, as often happens with magic, unexpected complications ensued—Blagden turned from black to ghostly white and acquired the power to foretell events. Since Evandar's death, Blagden has remained in the company of Queen Islanzadí and is renowned in the elven court for both a ribald wit and a serious manner.

BLASTED MOUNTAINS
SEE HADARAC DESERT.

BLÖDHGARM

Son of Ildrid the Beautiful and one of today's most powerful elven spellcasters. An experienced war commander and magical combatant, Blödhgarm is one of a group of twelve elves assigned to protect Eragon and Saphira. Blödhgarm's favored magical talent is his ability to alter his appearance to take on some of the physical attributes that he likes from an animal, such as a wolf. In addition to keen eyesight that rivals the penetrating gaze of the swiftest eagle, his body emits an intoxicating scent that attracts females of all races. His magical skills and fearlessness on the battlefield earned him the favor of Queen Islanzadí.

SEE LIOTHA.

BLOOD-OATH CELEBRATION

SEE AGAETÍ BLÖDHREN.

BOAR'S EYE

The monstrous whirlpool that forms between tides off the southwestern coast of Alagaësia, along the Southern Isles. The whirlpool is so gigantic its churning foam alone is the size of a large island. The Boar's Eye is the scourge of the bravest and most seaworthy sailor and can suck in entire fleets of ships from up to five miles away. The maelstrom is not without its strange beauty—a massive rainbow can often be seen descending from the sky into the whirlpool's misty heart. Traveling the Boar's Eye between low or high tides can give a false sense of security, as the area is then a seemingly harmless stretch of yellow foam. Only a few have entered the whirlpool and lived to tell of it, most recently Uthar, who sailed the *Dragon Wing* through it while escaping Galbatorix's navy.

BOLVEK

The Bolvek are an Urgal tribe led by a great Kull warrior, Nar Garzhvog. At the death of the evil Shade Durza, the Bolvek Urgals were released from the spells that had coerced them into serving the Empire. They realized their future was not secure so long as Galbatorix ruled and held his dreams of conquest, so they entered into an alliance with the Varden. In exchange for their assistance, Nasuada promised the Urgals new lands once the war with Galbatorix is won. Although the Varden hesitantly accepted the Bolvek as allies, they have since proved their bravery, dedication, and loyalty in battle and as Nasuada's personal guards, though skepticism remains among the ranks of the Varden.

SEE BATTLE OF THE BURNING PLAINS *AND* URGALS.

BONDEN

SEE DRAGON WING.

BOOK OF TOSK

The book of Tosk is the sacred work laying out the rules for the worshipers of the dark religion practiced at the weird rock formations of Helgrind.

BORROMEO CASTLE

SEE ABERON.

Braethan

A commander of a battalion of soldiers in Galbatorix's army.

Brand

The man appointed minister of trade under Lord Rishart, governor of Teirm. Brand is immune to bribery but has always tried to bend the law to suit his needs— the "worst sort of bureaucrat," the Dragon Rider Brom once said of him.

Bregan Hold

Situated on Mount Thardûr, this dwarf city in the Beor Mountains is the ancestral home of the Ingeitum clan. Built entirely of stone quarried from within the mountains, Bregan Hold rises in five levels to the pyramidal peak of Az Sindriznarrvel, the giant flameless lantern.

Brightsteel

A metal, known for its uncommon brilliance, smelted from an ore extracted from fragments of a shooting star. The ore was discovered in Alagaësia by the female elf and supreme swordsmith Rhunön. With this substance, Rhunön fashioned all the great Dragon Rider swords. Eragon and Saphira secured a nodule of brightsteel from beneath the roots of the Menoa tree. Eragon, under the guidance of Rhunön, fashioned the metal into his sword, Brisingr.

BRISINGR

The sword that Eragon christened with the ancient language word for "fire." Eragon risked the wrath of the sentient Menoa tree to obtain a store of the brightsteel buried beneath its roots. He brought the ore to Rhunön, who guided him in forging the greatest Dragon Rider sword of all.

SEE DRAGON RIDER SWORDS.

BRODDRING KINGDOM

The Broddrings were the first humans to settle Alagaësia and the youngest race on the continent. Their earliest known appearance was in 5596 AC, when twenty humans sailed from the south, landed near Surda, and exchanged gifts with dwarves before departing. It was nearly two thousand years before humans returned. King Palancar and his followers established the first permanent settlements in 7203 AC. According to elven lore, the humans came from an unknown homeland somewhere south of the Beor Mountains, their migration spurred by war and famine. Legend also holds that an evil race followed the humans to Alagaësia, the dark beings the elves named the Ra'zac—indeed, elves have also speculated that these fearsome creatures were the reason humans fled their homeland.

The fleet of ships under Palancar's command first attempted to land on the western coast of Alagaësia by the Spine mountain range, near the city of Teirm, but were blown back out to sea. The fleet made landfall on a bay to the south, where the pioneers established the first settlement, which they named Kuasta. A few years later, more ships carrying dark-skinned humans landed on the continent; this new wave of immigrants, today known as the wandering tribes, spread out along southern Alagaësia.

Palancar's people spent years searching for a route out of the Spine, eventually settling in the valley they named Palancar Valley, which became the center of the Broddring Kingdom. During this time, the humans discovered the elf city of Teirm. King Palancar met with the elves and negotiated the right of humans to settle on lands not inhabited by elves, dragons, or dwarves.

During Palancar's reign, humans expanded their borders, defeating Urgals and winning the territory that is today known as Therinsford. The conquest seemed to unhinge King Palancar. In his mad arrogance, Palancar lost his fear of the elves and Dragon Riders, tore up the treaty, and fought the elves for control of the region between the Spine and Du Weldenvarden. The Broddrings lost three great battles, but Palancar refused to concede. Rather than risk further defeats, Broddring nobles negotiated a separate peace accord with the elves, agreeing to dethrone and banish Palancar. In exchange, they were given control of Ilirea, the city that still remains the capital of the Broddring nation, although it is now under Galbatorix's control and known as Urû'baen. Palancar's banishment resulted in the construction of Ristvak-baen, the watchtower of the Riders. Palancar's fall was like a curse upon his house, with the deposed king murdered by his own son. It is said that descendants of the disgraced king still abide in the valley that bears his name.

The tragedy of Palancar's war spurred Anurin, elf leader of the Dragon Riders, to make the controversial decision to include the humans in the magical bond between elves and dragons, paving the way for the first human Dragon Rider.

King Angrenost, last true king of the Broddring Kingdom, was slain by Galbatorix and the Forsworn during their attack on Ilirea, and the Broddrings were absorbed by conquest into Galbatorix's Empire. However, as Galbatorix was solidifying his control, a group of humans led by Orrin seceded and formed the independent state of Surda. It is said that King Orrin can trace his ancestry to Thanebrand the Ring Giver, Palancar's successor, making Orrin a descendant of the Broddring royal bloodline.

See Surda.

BROKK

Father of Thorv.

BROM

Brom's father, Holcomb, and his mother, Nelda, originally lived in the secluded town of Kuasta. Both were illuminators who illustrated books and manuscripts. Brom, a Dragon Rider, whose own dragon was named Saphira, witnessed not only the downfall of his lineage but also its rebirth with a new young Rider—Eragon, his own son. Brom's honors include the highest awards the elf nation can give an outsider, the ring Aren and the title of elf-friend.

As a Dragon Rider, Brom was trained by Oromis in Ilirea. He was also close to his fellow Rider Morzan. The two became enemies when Morzan was corrupted by the rogue Rider Galbatorix, and Brom eventually slew Morzan. Selena, Morzan's consort, fell in love with Brom and their union bore Eragon.

An implacable foe of the Empire, Brom filled a vacuum when all was chaos: Galbatorix consolidating his Empire; the dwarves reeling from Galbatorix's attacks, which almost wiped out an entire clan; and a separatist movement of humans forming Surda. Brom was the first to organize the Riders' allies in exile and was one of the original founders of the Varden resistance. Brom not only secured the support of the elves but also convinced the dwarf king Hrothgar to allow the Varden to make their base in Farthen Dûr.

It is a matter of speculation why Brom did not become the Varden's leader, other than he was too independent and involved in his own endeavors. It was Brom who brought to the Varden the dragon egg that would hatch into Saphira. He negotiated the agreement with the elf queen Islanzadí as to how the dragon egg would be shared between elves and humans as well as training for the next Dragon Rider. Brom chose to live in Carvahall to be near his son, biding his time until the boy reached maturity and hiding his true identity under the guise of a village storyteller.

It would only be after Brom's death that Eragon would learn the Dragon Rider was his father, but the old Rider did fulfill his dream of initiating Eragon's training. Brom shared the history of the Riders and introduced him to the subtle magic of the ancient language and the clashing steel of combat swordsmanship. It was while trying to protect Eragon from the Ra'zac that Brom met his death.

Before the Siege of Feinster, Eragon finally learned the secrets of his parentage from the Rider Oromis and the dragon Glaedr. Saphira, who also knew the secret, gave Eragon the gift of a memory vision Brom left with her, which spoke of many things and left his son with the advice that Eragon protect his loved ones and that, if Galbatorix still lived, there would be no peace for Eragon and Saphira until the tyrant's death.

See Brom's tomb.

BROM IS NAMED AFTER AN AMERICAN
FANTASY ARTIST.

Brom's tomb

Upon Brom's death at the hands of the Ra'zac—during the fight in which Brom saved Eragon's life—Eragon used magic to erect a sandstone tomb not far from the Empire city of Dras-Leona. What Eragon built from stone, Saphira then transformed into diamond, forever keeping Brom's mortal remains in a pristine state untouched by decay. Brom's old friend Jeod Longshanks complimented Eragon and Saphira, saying they had made a tomb even a dwarf king would envy, but he cautioned that vandals might try to extract the diamond. Eragon decided he would one day return and place magic spells around Brom's resting place to protect it from grave robbers.

BRUGH

One of the horses belonging to Garrow of Carvahall.

BULLRIDGE

This small town on the western side of the Ramr River is the closest settlement to the Hadarac Desert.

BURAGH

This large dwarf city is near the northern edge of the Beor Mountains, in proximity to the Hadarac Desert.

BURNING PLAINS

Situated where the border of Surda meets the eastern stretch of the Jiet River, this large area of peat deposits was once accidentally set aflame by dragons during a battle between the Riders and the Forsworn. Ever since, the plain has been burning and blackening the skies with smoke and toxic fumes, rendering the land uninhabitable. The ancient language name for the Burning Plains is Du Völlar Eldrvarya.

SEE BATTLE OF THE BURNING PLAINS.

BYRD

The husband of Felda, father of several children, and a popular citizen of Carvahall. During the Empire's siege, Byrd stood watch for soldiers attempting to sneak into Carvahall during nightfall. While on watch, he was ambushed and killed by the traitorous Sloan. Byrd's widow eventually accompanied Carvahall refugees on the journey to safe haven in Surda.

Mandel, Byrd and Felda's eldest son, also made the journey to Surda but fell in with a bad crowd. After Mandel gambled away the few remaining family valuables, Felda sought Roran's help. Roran, the leader of the refugees, wisely engaged Mandel in constructive tasks, making him his personal messenger and a watchman for the villagers, which helped the restless youth become a responsible member of the community.

Cadoc

The horse that Brom bought for Eragon from the dealer Haberth in Therinsford as they fled from Carvahall. Eragon named the horse Cadoc after his grandfather, Garrow and Selena's father.

THE NAME CADOC IS *KODAK* SPELLED
BACKWARD BUT WITH *C*'S.

CANTOS

A small village within the Empire's territory that Galbatorix ordered destroyed for allegedly harboring traitors. Galbatorix directed Murtagh, son of Morzan, to oversee the village's destruction. When Murtagh heard that the villagers would not be offered amnesty, he tried to escape the Empire. The village was nonetheless razed, with no survivors left behind.

CARDUS WEED

The favored plant for pipe smoking among the races of Alagaësia. Smoking cardus weed was a pastime popularized by the dwarves.

CARETAKERS

Maintaining the sacred bond between dragons and their Riders are the Caretakers, Iduna and Nëya, two beautiful and nearly identical female elves who embody the exalted values of the Riders. The pair look so much alike that they can only be distinguished by their hair—one has black hair, the other silver. Their bodies are covered with rainbow-colored tattoos that, when they stand together, form a dragon. Once a century, the Caretakers perform the ritual of the Agaetí Blödhren to honor and renew the ancient pact. During the most recent celebration, the Caretakers sanctified Eragon, granting him the grace and physical skills of an adult elf and hastening the transformation that would normally take years for a human Rider. This gift from the dragons was deemed vital in helping Eragon bring freedom and justice to Alagaësia.

CARN

A thin, nervous Varden magician who became both a trusted friend and spell-caster for Roran when Roran came under the command of the Varden's Martland Redbeard. Although Carn struggles to cast his spells, his greatest strength is his ability to worm his way into opponents' minds.

CARSAIB

See Durza.

CARVAHALL

A village, nestled in Palancar Valley amid the Spine, whose economy included surrounding farms. The village's natural isolation forced the townspeople to be self-sufficient. Residents of historic interest include Brom and Eragon, and it was here that the dragon egg bearing Saphira hatched under Eragon's protection.

Carvahall finally came under attack from the Ra'zac and Galbatorix's soldiers. The townspeople bravely resisted, forming a militia and constructing defenses along its borders. Although the villagers repelled a number of attacks, it became clear they couldn't withstand the siege forever. Many villagers banded together and escaped to the safety of Surda. Carvahall was finally destroyed by the Empire soldiers, and anyone who remained is believed to have been executed.

CASTLE ILIREA

The elven castle within the ancient city of Ilirea, now known as Urû'baen, capital of Galbatorix's Empire.

See Galbatorix, Ilirea, *and* Urû'baen.

CAWLEY

A farmer on Nost Creek in the valley outside Carvahall. Cawley's farm was intended as a refuge for Carvahall children during the Empire's attack, but a blockade of soldiers and the arrival of Ra'zac shattered that plan. Farmer Cawley's fate is unknown.

CELBEDEIL

One of the most stunning architectural structures of the dwarf nation and its greatest temple. Celbedeil is situated atop the terraced surface city of Tarnag. Its walls are speckled with gems of every color and covered by ivy vines, and it's replete with statuary depicting dwarven gods and mythic battles between monsters and deities. An ethereal aroma of flowers and incense pervades the temple. Also noteworthy is a famed temple mural—made of carved plates of marble that were fired and fitted into a seamless whole—that depicts key historic events, including the race's exodus out of the Hadarac Desert to the Beor Mountains, the carving of Isidar Mithrim, the first meeting with the elves, the war between dragons and elves that shook the land, and the coronation of dwarf kings.

See TARNAG.

CELDIN

An elf from Ceris.

CERANTHOR

An elf king, the subject of a poem included in the *Domia abr Wyrda*.

Ceris

A small elven outpost for sentinels. Ceris is stationed along the eastern edge of Du Weldenvarden, near the Edda River.

Ceunon

A human city, formerly under control of the Empire, at the western border of Du Weldenvarden. When the elves officially joined the war against Galbatorix, Ceunon was the first city they aimed to conquer. The people of Ceunon had earned the elves' wrath for sneaking into Du Weldenvarden to cut down the sacred trees, using the timber to construct weapons of war for Galbatorix's army. Lord Tarrant, ruler of Ceunon, barricaded himself in a fortified tower when the city was attacked and taken by the elven army. At present, Ceunon remains under elven control.

Chronicles of Ingothold, The

See Ingothold.

Cithrí

Situated along the northern border of Surda and one of that kingdom's five major cities.

City of Eternal Twilight

See Tronjheim.

CLANMEET

The name for the gathering of dwarf clans, during which the new ruler of the nation is chosen. The selection of a new ruler is announced with the drumbeat of the Drums of Derva.

CLOVIS

A stout, bearded fisherman from Narda and owner of the barges *Merrybell*, *Edeline*, and *Red Boar*. Clovis was deceived by Roran into sailing Carvahall villagers from Narda to Teirm. Despite realizing he had been tricked, Clovis kept his bargain and helped the villagers make it to Teirm.

CONVOCATIONS

See Nuala.

COUNCIL OF ELDERS

An advisory group to the elected Varden leader, which also contributes to the running of the government. After Ajihad's death, the Council of Elders hoped to install his daughter, Nasuada, as a puppet leader whom they could control. Eragon, however, undermined the council when he publicly swore his fealty to Nasuada herself, not to the Varden (and thus not to the council). Jörmundur, Ajihad's second in command, is on the Council of Elders. Other members include Elessari, one of the oldest members of the original Varden movement, who has grown corrupt during her long tenure; Falberd, renowned for both his arrogance and devious ways; Umérth, who uses his power solely to advance his personal agenda; and Sabrae, a cunning political strategist who is often clumsy, though, in her attempted manipulations of others.

CRAGS OF TEL'NAEÍR

This majestic mass of rocks near Ellesméra was once the refuge of the Rider Oromis and his dragon, Glaedr. During his training, Eragon and Saphira spent much time here under the tutelage of Oromis and Glaedr.

SEE OROMIS AND GLAEDR.

CRIPPLE WHO IS WHOLE, THE

SEE OROMIS AND GLAEDR.

CURSE OF THE NAMED BLADE

The myth that warriors will be cursed if they win renown in battle with any weapon other than their own named weapons. The Varden weapon master, Fredric, mentioned this curse to Eragon when the Rider came to him for a sword after the loss of Zar'roc to Murtagh.

D

Dagshelgr Invocation

An elven rite of spring designed to ensure the health and fertility of the forest. All across Du Weldenvarden, elves sing to the trees, other plants, and the forest creatures. The rite's alluring spells can be dangerous for mortals. "Without us, Du Weldenvarden would be half its size," Arya has noted of the magical union elves have with their forest realm.

See Du Weldenvarden.

Dahwar

A Surdan, son of Kedar and seneschal to King Orrin. Dahwar's duties include serving in King Orrin's stead when the king is away on official business.

DALGON

A large dwarf city within the heart of the Beor Mountains. On an infamous note, Dalgon was where much of the planning was conducted for the ambush of Eragon and his guard at Farthen Dûr.

DAMITHA

An old friend of Arya, this beautiful female elf is captain of the guard in Sílthrim.

DANCE OF SNAKE AND CRANE
See RIMGAR.

DARET

A small, ominous-looking village in the Empire situated by the Ninor River. Daret is under constant siege by various raiders, including packs of Urgals. The resistance in the besieged riverfront town is led by Trevor, a veteran warrior and strategist and a former soldier in Galbatorix's army. Brom and Eragon won over the suspicious Trevor and purchased supplies in Daret during their journey in search of the Ra'zac.

DARK GATES
See HELGRIND.

DÄTHEDR

A tall, lithe, silver-haired elf lord and advisor to Queen Islanzadí and friend to the queen's daughter, Arya. A respected member of the elven government and a formidable warrior, Däthedr is usually at the queen's side during official functions, government meetings, and war councils.

DAUTH

A Surdan port along the southwestern coast of Alagaësia and home to a number of famed artisans of the Wandering Tribes. When the villagers from Carvahall fled the Empire because of the attacks on their homes, they found safe haven in Dauth, where Lady Alarice offered them aid and refuge.

DAZHGRA

A powerful Urgal shaman and member of the Bolvek tribe. Dazhgra's powers include control over elemental forces, and his skills are considered superior to those of most Varden magicians.

DEED OF GËDA, THE

An epic of the elves. It was among the numerous materials Oromis gave to Eragon in Ellesméra.

DEEP DWELLERS

Dwarves who cannot abide the surface world and choose to live deep underground. Most deep dwellers prefer to live below Farthen Dûr and Tronjheim, as they can come out and still feel underground, surrounded as they are by the volcanic hollow where the capital city stands.

DELLANIR

The elf queen who preceded Evandar. It was Queen Dellanir who had the wisdom to ensure that Dragon Riders were autonomous from any monarch or kingdom and that they have access to the wonders of Du Weldenvarden.

See Dragon Riders.

DELVA

A form of gold nodule found in the Beor Mountains. Delva is so prized by the dwarves that the word itself is used as a term of endearment.

DELWIN

A farmer in Carvahall and the husband of Lenna. During the Empire's invasion, Delwin proved himself a capable watchman and fighter, contributing to the planning of the village defenses and personally killing several Empire soldiers.

Lenna was an early supporter of evacuating Carvahall in order to spare as many lives as possible. Elmund, the couple's ten-year-old son and the youngest of their six children, was slain during the siege.

DEMPTON

A friendly miller in Therinsford who apprenticed Roran.

DERÛND

The father of the dwarf clan chief Ûndin.

DERWOOD

A soldier in the Empire's army who was quick to gossip about Galbatorix's troop placements and other sensitive matters.

DEYNOR

Ajihad's predecessor as Varden leader. The Dragon Rider Brom, while in hiding from Galbatorix, made a secret trip to the Varden refuge in Farthen Dûr to reveal to Deynor that he was still alive. It was also Deynor who allowed the spellcasters the Twins to join the Varden—a decision that proved disastrous when the pair ultimately revealed themselves to be traitors and agents of the Empire.

Domia Abr Wyrda

A book by Heslant the Monk; the title translates as *Dominance of Fate*. Considered the most complete history of Alagaësia, the work was banned by Galbatorix, who declared it blasphemy and ordered the author's execution. Galbatorix's destruction of copies of the book, and the obvious risk it holds for anyone owning it, makes this among the rarest books in Alagaësia. Eragon received a copy as a gift from Jeod, which he cherished.

See Arcaena *and* Jeod.

Dóndar

The tenth dwarf king.

Dormnad

A Varden spy stationed within the key Empire city of Gil'ead. Dormnad's ability to blend in with the local populace made him privy to gossip about the movement of Galbatorix's troops. At one point, Eragon was referred to Dormnad to learn the location of the Varden's sanctuary.

Doru Araeba

The capital city of the Dragon Riders shortly after their secession from elven influence.

See Vrael *and* Vroengard.

Dragon Riders

Millennia before the arrival of humans and Urgals, the conflicts of Alagaësia centered on the newly arrived elf race and the dragons, the continent's most ancient race. The turning point in the war between dragons and elves came when a young elf named Eragon discovered an abandoned dragon egg. Eragon bonded with the hatchling, Bid'Daum, and they became ambassadors between their races. Not only was peace ultimately achieved, but Eragon and Bid'Daum became the first Dragon Riders, the knightly lineage that would commemorate the peace pact as guardians of peace and security. Once the exclusive province of dragons and elves, this pact would later include humans. Dwarves, because of their natural suspicion of others, did not even request to be part of the brotherhood of Dragon Riders.

It is believed by some that the Riders' autonomy, assured by Queen Dellanir, bore the seeds of their eventual fall (which, however, came thousands of years later). Certainly the fall finally came from one of their own. The Dragon Rider Galbatorix, distraught at the death of his dragon, felt betrayed when he was denied a new dragon. The grieving Rider plotted vengeance and corrupted other Riders, the so-called Thirteen Forsworn, who joined his cause and began the war that led to the Fall of the Dragon Riders.

Mentored by the Dragon Rider Brom, Eragon represents a new generation of Riders, the first in over a hundred years. As with all Riders, Eragon and his dragon communicate telepathically.

See Forsworn, Galbatorix, Indlvarn, *and* Tuatha du Orothrim.

Dragon Rider swords

According to the Varden weapon master, Fredric, every great warrior must wield a sword that has a name, whether given by the warrior or by the bards who sing of the swordsman's exploits. More than a mere weapon, a named sword is the essence of a warrior, making it unthinkable to go into combat with any other weapon. For a Dragon Rider, a named sword has even greater meaning, symbolizing both the individual and the proud lineage of the order. Also, according to the Rider Oromis, all Riders' swords have a jewel in the pommel in which the Rider stores energy. The female elf Rhunön fashioned all the Dragon Rider swords from brightsteel. Her famous swords include the following:

Arvindr: One of the few remaining Rider swords within the elves' possession. It is located in the elven city of Nädindel.

Támerlein: Another of the remaining Riders' swords in the possession of the elves. Imbued with a rich green hue and topped by a large emerald, this sword was made larger than normal and designed to be wielded with two hands. The powerful sword was originally crafted for Arva, the elven Dragon Rider who, when mortally wounded in battle, gave the sword to his sister, Naudra. When Naudra also fell from her own battle wounds, the sword came under the protection of Lord Fiolr of the House Valtharos, who offered the sword to Eragon for use in battle. Eragon, realizing the Támerlein was a poor fit for him, declined.

Undbitr: The original blue sword of Brom, which was lost in the course of the many battles that marked the downfall of the Riders.

Naegling: The golden and bronze sword of Oromis, Rider of Glaedr, marked at the hilt by a giant golden jewel that stores vast magical energy. The sword, which saw the Rider through many successful battles, was lost after Oromis's death.

Zar'roc: The most infamous Dragon Rider sword. The name means "Misery," and the sword was created for the Dragon Rider Morzan before he became the dark disciple of Galbatorix. The sword is blood-red; the pommel is set with a ruby for storing energy. With Morzan's death, the sword was taken by Brom, who passed it on to Eragon. Zar'roc was later taken from Eragon by Murtagh (who had been forced to declare his allegiance to Galbatorix) during the Battle of the Burning Plains.

Brisingr: After the Fall of the Riders, the elf smith Rhunön swore never to forge another Rider sword. Presented with Eragon's plight, however, she circumvented her oath by guiding Eragon, who fashioned the sword himself. One of its unique (and unintended) magical properties is the ability to burst into a blue flame when Eragon utters the word *Brisingr* while holding it. This color matches the scales of Eragon's dragon, Saphira. Eragon used it for the first time in the Battle of Feinster.

> RIDER SWORDS ARE MADE OF METALLIC GLASS, WHICH IS A REAL SUBSTANCE THAT IS MUCH STRONGER THAN REGULAR STEEL.

DRAGONS

The oldest and wisest race to inhabit Alagaësia, dragons are believed to be as old as the continent. In dwarven myth, the brother gods Urûr, god of the air and heavens, and Morgothal, god of fire, combined their talents to create the dragon race. Dragons are highly intelligent, fire-breathing creatures (gaining the latter ability at five to six months old), capable of flying great distances. Dragons' scales are shiny as polished gems, and they come in every color of the rainbow. A dragon never stops growing, and a mature dragon's wingspan can easily measure a hundred feet across. Dragons use a powerful, instinctual magic that even they cannot fully predict or control.

The seminal event of dragon history was the Dragon War against the elves. The five-year struggle ended with a peace pact and ushered in the lineage of Dragon Riders who kept the peace for the next 2,600 years.

The bond between a dragon and his or her Rider is immutable; their closeness is typified by their telepathic communication. Although virtually wiped out during Galbatorix's rise to power, dragons live on in their Eldunarí, a secret revealed after the Siege of Feinster.

SEE DRAGONS AND RIDERS IN THE APPENDIX. SEE ALSO ELDUNARÍ.

THE GEMLIKE SCALES OF CHRISTOPHER PAOLINI'S DRAGONS WERE IN-
SPIRED IN PART BY THE IRIDESCENT FEATHERS OF THE HUMMINGBIRD.
HUMMINGBIRDS ARE ALSO ONE OF THE FEW CREATURES THAT HAVE
COLORS AS PURE AND BRIGHT AS A DRAGON'S.

DRAGON WAR
SEE DU FYRN SKULBLAKA.

DRAGON WING
Kinnell, a master shipwright, was responsible for the *Dragon Wing*, one of the finest sailing ships ever built. It was owned by the Blackmoor Shipping Company, a front for the Empire. Bonden, a sailor who assisted in the theft of this prized sailing ship, joined Jeod Longshanks and other escapees on the journey to Surda.

DRAIL
An assassin trained "in the dark uses of magic" whose attempt to kill Nasuada with a metal dart was thwarted by Elva. The short, bearded, plain-looking Drail committed suicide by magic upon his capture by Nasuada's warriors.
SEE BLACK HAND.

Dras-Leona

A sprawling Empire city on the eastern edge of Leona Lake, infamous for its poverty, flourishing slave trade, and dark religion. Dras-Leona is one of the most poorly planned cities in Alagaësia; the roads leading in are often crowded with farmers bringing their goods to the city market.

An atmosphere of evil pervades Dras-Leona. In fact, the city was built because of its proximity to the rock spires of Helgrind, a few miles to the east. Despite poor city planning and ramshackle neighborhoods, the city defenses are well engineered and include a large wall patrolled by sentries and archers. Dras-Leona's ruler, Lord Marcus Tábor, is a loyal servant of the Empire but has incurred the wrath of Galbatorix.

The most significant structure in Dras-Leona, which can be seen as one approaches the city gates, is a cathedral whose design emulates the vertical spires of Helgrind. Situated in the physical center of the rambling city, the cathedral is the heart of a religion whose practitioners drink human blood and make flesh offerings. Many of the priests are missing body parts due to their belief that offering up their own flesh makes them less attached to the physical world.

See Helgrind.

Dream Well

A magical phenomenon found in Mani's Caves.
See Beor Mountains.

Drums of Derva

See clanmeet.

Du Fells Nángoröth

The mountain range in the Hadarac Desert where wild dragons traditionally mated, raised their young, and passed into the void. The name means "The Blasted Mountains."

Du Fyrn Skulblaka

The first war in Alagaësia's history marked a turning point for all life on the continent. Du Fyrn Skulblaka pitted native dragons against the elves who had migrated to Alagaësia. The war's cause was a tragic misunderstanding—the elves, who are superior hunters, assumed dragons were wild beasts, not the highly evolved sentient beings they are. When some elves tracked and killed them for sport, the dragons declared war. Both races were equal in cunning and ferocity. Casualties mounted on both sides. Locked in combat, the opponents raced toward mutual extinction, neither gaining an advantage.

The turning point came when a young elf named Eragon discovered a dragon egg and protected it. Eragon and Bid'Daum, the hatchling dragon, became inseparable, and theirs was the first bond between dragons and elves. With the end of the war, the Dragon Riders were formed and charged with maintaining peace and security for all.

Du Namar Aurboda

King Galbatorix rose to power with the destruction of the Dragon Riders. For dragons, the bitterest betrayal of the great lineage was the thirteen dragons who joined Galbatorix and the Thirteen Forsworn. In retaliation, dragons opposing Galbatorix stripped those renegade dragons of their spoken and true names. This powerful act of magic became known as Du Namar Aurboda, or The Banishing of the Names. The spell was unforgiving—without names, the dragons were without purpose and many were reduced to madness and the brute level of animals.

See Forsworn.

DÛRGRIMST

Referring to the dwarf clan, *dûrgrimst* literally means "our hall" or "our home."

DÛRGRIMST INGEITUM

A powerful dwarf clan known for its skilled smith work. Many kings have come from its ranks, including Hrothgar and Orik. Eragon himself was made an honorary member by Hrothgar, a gesture that bound Eragon to the clan and allows him to attend dwarven councils.

See Dwarf Clans *in the appendix.*

DÛRGRIMSTVREN

In the Dwarvish language, "clan war." It has been two centuries since the last dûrgrimstvren, although tensions between the clans recently came to the boiling point.

See clanmeet.

DÛROK ORNTHROND

The craftsman who devoted his life to shaping the great gemstone sculpture of the dwarf nation, Isidar Mithrim. His name means "Eagle-eye."

Durza

A sorcerer whose life story is a tragic example not only of evil begetting evil but also of the deadly risks inherent in the use of magic. Durza began life as Carsaib, a young man who lived with his parents in the empty plains after their tribe called his father an oath breaker and abandoned them. After his parents were murdered by strangers, the distraught youth wandered the desert. He was near death when discovered by the hermit wizard Haeg, who nicknamed him "Desert Rat." Haeg nursed him back to health and trained him in sorcery. When a spell backfired and crippled Haeg, it was his apprentice's turn to care for the ailing hermit. However, not long after his recovery, Haeg was murdered by bandits. Carsaib, seeking revenge, summoned spirits to do his will, but they in turn possessed him, transforming him into Durza the Shade. Durza became a powerful figure in the Empire, second only to his master, Galbatorix.

A tall and powerfully built figure with blood-red hair that contrasted with his translucent skin, Durza was not only a great magician but also a skilled warrior and military leader who was assigned the most vital matters of the Empire. In a rare failure, Durza missed by seconds the chance to regain the dragon egg stolen from Galbatorix, which the elf princess Arya magically transported to the Spine. Although Durza captured and tortured Arya, she did not reveal the whereabouts of the egg or any secrets of the Varden.

The Empire went on the offensive after discovering the Varden sanctuary in Farthen Dûr, within the Beor Mountains. Durza used magic to gain control of an army of Urgals that led the attack on the Varden. While in fierce combat with Eragon, Durza was destroyed when a thrust of Eragon's sword pierced his heart, releasing the spirits and ending his reign of terror.

See Arya.

DUSAN
See ELF CHILDREN.

"DU SILBENA DATIA"
An elven song celebrating the sea.

DÛTHMER
One of the guards for the dwarf clan chief Ûndin.

DU VÖLLAR ELDRVARYA
See BURNING PLAINS.

DU VRANGR GATA
The organization of spellcasters who serve the Varden but whose actions are unpredictable. The name means "The Wandering Path."
See TRIANNA *and* TWINS.

DU WELDENVARDEN
The largest forest in Alagaësia, Du Weldenvarden ("The Guarding Forest") spreads across much of the continent's northern area. When Eragon first ap-

proached this region, he saw it as a ridge of green that became a virtual emerald sea as he got closer—*Like another world,* he thought.

Thousands of years of elven spellcasting in Du Weldenvarden has resulted in trees of incredible size, notably oaks, beeches, pines, and maples. The forest is home to most of the elf population, and elven settlements include seven villages and cities, notably Ellesméra, the capital. The elves have become guardians of the forest and have placed magical wards around it that prevent anyone or anything from entering it by magical means.

SEE LIOTHA *AND* MENOA TREE.

DU WYRDFELL
SEE FORSWORN.

DVALAR
A spellweaver of old, dedicated to studying and inventing defensive spells, Dvalar is known for his special spells of protection.

DWARVEN BURIAL RITES
Although there is much secrecy connected to the burial rites of dwarves, it is known that dwarves believe they are people of stone and that bodies of the dead must be sealed in stone. Only then can dwarves be assured that their spirits reach the Hall of Helzvog. In the passageways under Farthen Dûr exist the chambers in which dwarves are entombed in the ancient custom.

SEE AJIHAD'S TOMB.

DWARVEN CREATION MYTH

Dwarves believe that their gods vanquished giants who once ruled the world. Helzvog, the god of stone, defied the other gods and secretly created the first dwarf. There was great jealousy, and only Kílf restrained herself as the other gods created their own races: Sindri made human beings, and the brothers Urûr and Morgothal brought forth the dragons.

DWARVES

Along with dragons, the oldest sentient race in Alagaësia. Dwarves have an innate knowledge of magic and are renowned in metallurgy, blacksmithing, and other fields. Dwarves believe they were created "from the roots of a mountain" by Helzvog, the god of stone. Their word for dwarf is *knurla*, which literally means "one of stone." The dwarven pantheon of omnipotent beings includes Kílf, goddess of rivers and seas; Sindri, goddess of the earth; the brothers Urûr, god of air and heavens, and Morgothal, god of fire; and Güntera, king of the gods.

The foundation of dwarven culture is the clan system: thirteen clans, each ruled by a powerful chief. But all dwarves are ruled by a king elected by the clans at a clanmeet, a gathering that can involve months of deliberation and debate before a vote is cast.

The dwarves, who originally dwelt in the verdant lands of what would become the Hadarac Desert, migrated to the Beor Mountains when the climate became inhospitable. In that mighty mountain range, they began excavating a vast network of tunnels and building magnificent cities that are among the wonders of Alagaësia. Eragon himself has observed that dwarves can reshape granite with the same degree of skill with which elves reshape plants. Their skill as stoneworkers is evident in the tunnels and passageways of the gigantic volcanic crater of Farthen Dûr, while the capital of Tronjheim situated there is a mountain-sized city that took generations to build and could house the nation in an emergency. The greatest work of dwarven craftsmanship is Isidar Mithrim, which crowns Tronjheim's pyramidal heights, a rose-colored star sapphire sixty feet across that Dûrok Ornthrond took fifty-seven years to extract from stone and sculpt to perfection.

Despite its great accomplishments, the race has destructive impulses, as even King Orik noted in the course of the clanmeet that elected him. Dwarves are generally contemptuous of the outside world, and a regret of Orik's was that when dragons and elves formed the Dragon Riders, the dwarves did not ask to be included. But even Orik, recalling the legends of giants who once ruled the earth, has referred to humans and elves as the "giants" of the present age, "stomping about with their big feet and casting us in endless shadows."

SEE DWARVEN BURIAL RITES AND DWARF CLANS IN THE APPENDIX. SEE ALSO ISIDAR MITHRIM AND TRONJHEIM.

THE DWARF CAVES WERE PARTIALLY INSPIRED BY THE CARLSBAD CAVERNS IN NEW MEXICO AND THE LEWIS AND CLARK CAVERNS IN MONTANA.

EARNË

An elven poet whose writings are often quoted as examples to wayward youths.

EASTCROFT

A medium-sized farming village of the Empire twenty miles north of Melian. Eastcroft is a popular stop for travelers journeying between the Empire's southernmost towns and cities. Eragon stopped here while traveling alone after the defeat of the Ra'zac in Helgrind; Arya found him at the wayfarers' house.

EDEL

The lord mentioned in the song "Sweet Aethrid o' Dauth."
See AETHRID.

EDELINE

One of the three barges that Roran and the villagers of Carvahall took from Narda.

EDOC'SIL

See UTGARD MOUNTAIN.

EDRIC

Varden captain, one of Nasuada's commanders. In an infamous incident, Roran defied Edric's orders during battle. Roran feared that Edric was leading the men to slaughter and shifted tactics midstream in order to save the men from massacre and win the battle. Although Nasuada relieved Edric of his command, Roran's insubordination resulted in a punishment of fifty lashes.

See RORAN.

EDUR CARTHUNGAVË

See SPINE, THE.

EDUR ITHINDRA

South of Helgrind, this former elven stronghold and watchtower today lies in ruins. The crumbling tower has since become the home of the cloistered hermit Tenga.

See TENGA.

EDURNA

An elf from Ceris.

EKKSVAR

One of the guards for the dwarf clan chief Ûndin.

ELAIN

Horst's wife and the mother of Albriech and Baldor. A small, willowy woman, she is a mother figure to Eragon and Katrina, Roran's wife. She was five months pregnant during the siege of Carvahall and ill and overdue during the Siege of Feinster.

ELDER RACES

General term for the ancient races of Alagaësia.

ELDUNARÍ

One of the great secrets of Alagaësia is the Eldunarí, also known as a dragon's heart of hearts. This gemlike object is a physical part of a dragon, buried deep within the chest area. Within it, the dragon can store an immense amount of energy, as well as its consciousness. Every dragon is born with a dormant and colorless Eldunarí. As the dragon ages, the Eldunarí grows in both size and energy-storing capacity. A dragon may, if it so chooses, disgorge its heart of hearts, which then allows the dragon to exist in two places at once: in its original body and in the Eldunarí. This was often useful when a dragon and its Rider had to travel apart. If the dragon keeps its heart of hearts within its body, the gemlike object will dissolve upon the dragon's death.

An Eldunarí is a source of vulnerability for a dragon, for whoever possesses a heart of hearts holds a dragon's life in his hands. If an Eldunarí breaks, the dragon will instantly die, both in mind and in body.

Before they formed their pact with the elves, dragons traditionally hid a store of disgorged Eldunarí within Du Fells Nángoröth, the mountains of the Hadarac Desert. When the Riders created a repository for the Eldunarí on the island of Vroengard, dragons entrusted this most important part of themselves to their Riders. When a dragon's Rider passed away, the dragon often either smashed its own heart of hearts or, if its body was no more, arranged for someone else to do it for them. But not always. A fair number of dragons continued to live on and serve the Riders as best they could from their heart of hearts. The elven Rider Oromis has observed that the question of how a living Eldunarí acquires its energy is a mystery—is it similar to how plants absorb sunlight, or does it feed off the energy of other living things? No one knows, not even the dragons.

Upon the Fall of the Riders, the store of Eldunarí on Vroengard—in the city of Doru Araeba—came into Galbatorix's possession. It is believed that the Eldunarí of the wild dragons of old and the dragons slain by the Forsworn are the source of much of Galbatorix's power.

SEE INDLVARN.

ELESSARI

SEE COUNCIL OF ELDERS.

ELF CHILDREN

Unlike other races, the virtually immortal elves rarely reproduce. Thus, elf children are rare creatures, revered for their natural grace and the beauty of their glowing skin and their eyes that emanate a soft light. The most recent children are Alanna and Dusan, who currently live in Ellesméra.

ELF-FRIEND

The special title bestowed, along with the mystical ring Aren, upon outsiders who have rendered great service for the elf nation. In recent times, those honored include Brom and Eragon.

ELF SHIPS

Fashioned of birch bark or other materials, elven sailing vessels are masterpieces of construction and a wonder to behold. The elves magically sing their ships into a seamless whole of incredible strength and lightness, as they have done ever since they first came to Alagaësia.

ELLESMÉRA

The capital city of the elves lies hidden deep within Du Weldenvarden and is home to the royal family and most of the elven population.

Ellesméra is heavily guarded by elf sentinels and an intricate series of magical defenses. Those seeking entrance must request permission from Gilderien the

Wise, city guardian and wielder of the White Flame of Vándil. To an outsider, it would initially appear as if no city existed, only forest. However, this is a city built not of bricks and stones, but of the forest trees. The elves use magic to transform trees into elegant, organic structures.

Although humans have settled on the western edge of Du Weldenvarden, only the elves know the secrets of the deep forest, which is wilder than even the rugged Spine. The forest holds many dangers, including, it is said, ancient spells whose power still lingers.

After being wounded in the Battle of Farthen Dûr, Eragon is summoned to Ellesméra for training. There he and Saphira are mentored by Oromis and Glaedr.

SEE AGAETÍ BLÖDHREN *AND* MENOA TREE.

ELMUND
SEE DELWIN.

ELVA
Also known as "Farseer," this young female member of the Varden is a heart-breaking example of well-intended magic gone awry. As a baby, Elva lived within Farthen Dûr in the care of an old woman, Greta. During one of Eragon's visits, Greta offered the baby to be blessed by the young hero. Eragon gave her his blessing, and Saphira touched her brow, leaving there a silvery star-shaped patch. He assumed that only happiness would follow, but Elva began to rapidly mature— eating constantly, growing far faster than a normal child, and manifesting the strange ability to predict others' suffering. Although her words are those of an adult, she speaks with the voice of a child. Her eyes are violet. Greta consulted with Angela the herbalist, who sent the werecat Solembum to alert Nasuada.

Nasuada asked Angela to keep an eye on Elva, to make sure she didn't become dangerous. Meanwhile, during his stay in Ellesméra, Eragon learned from Oromis that in his haste and inexperience in the use of the ancient language, he had bestowed a curse, not a blessing. Elva can sense and predict pain in those around her and feels compelled to shield them from it. If she resists the urge, she becomes physically ill.

Nasuada decided that Elva's strange powers to predict pain and suffering could be used in the service of the Varden. Elva saved Nasuada from Drail, a Black Hand assassin, tackling the Varden leader before a metal dart struck her. When Eragon returned to the Varden after his training in Ellesméra, he attempted to remove Elva's curse but was only partly successful. Now Elva can still sense pain but can choose to ignore it—which makes her all the more dangerous.

See Angela the herbalist.

ELVES

Their ancient origins are shrouded in mystery. Elves came to Alagaësia from a place they call Alalëa, although no one knows where, or what, this land is. Magical beings with a reverence for nature, elves tragically and ironically first assumed the native dragons were dumb beasts. This misunderstanding led to Du Fyrn Skulblaka, the war that ended only when the elf Eragon found a dragon egg and bonded with the hatchling, Bid'Daum. The two not only helped win a cessation of war but also forged a bond between elves and dragons that kept peace for thousands of years. The war against Galbatorix and the Empire forced the elves to retreat into Du Weldenvarden, where they remained in hiding for a century.

The elves, who once had a life span similar to that of human beings, are practically immortal, although vulnerable to physical injury. They are known as the "fair folk" because of their physical beauty, as well as their love of beauty in all its manifestations. Elves use the ancient language in song and music to encourage plant life to grow into the shapes they desire, forming the very living spaces of

their cities. Elves often use their powers to reshape their own physical appearance, sometimes
dramatically. Despite their sublime and holistic
ways, their natural agility, speed, and strength
make them superb fighters, and they are masters
of swordsmanship and horsemanship. Indeed,
Eragon has observed that elves seem to move
too quickly and fluidly for beings of flesh and
blood.

As students and scholars of nature, elves believe in immutable rules that govern the world. They do not believe in gods and creation stories. Miracles can be
explained, the elves believe, and they assert there is no known example of any
god breaking the rules that govern the world. As Oromis once taught Eragon, a
major difference between elves and dwarves is that dwarves have a belief system
that is predicated more on faith than reason.

The elf nation is today led by the beautiful queen Islanzadí. Her daughter,
Arya, was instrumental in Eragon discovering the dragon egg that bore Saphira.
Arya has fought alongside the young Rider and his dragon in many battles. In-
deed, Eragon, like his father Brom, is considered a friend of the elf nation.

See Arya, Du Weldenvarden, Ellesméra, Islanzadí, and Menoa tree.

Empire, The

The collection of Alagaësian lands under the control of King Galbatorix,
spanning the western half of the continent. When Galbatorix seized power over
the Broddring nation, many humans, fearing his tyrannical rule, defected and
formed the independent state of Surda. Their prescience has been confirmed by
the weary citizens of the Empire, who chafe at the brutal regime, with its massive
standing army and onerous taxes.

Endless Staircase

See Vol Turin.

Eoam

A coastal village on the Southern Isle of Beirland.

Eragon

The young elf who, during the war between elves and dragons, discovered a dragon egg and decided to protect it. Bid'Daum, the hatchling white dragon, and Eragon became as one, and their friendship opened communications between the races, which ended the war. Eragon and Bid'Daum are considered the first in the long line of Dragon Riders.

See Du Fyrn Skulblaka.

Eragon

Eragon, son of the Dragon Rider Brom and the former assassin Selena, was raised by his aunt Marian and uncle Garrow, along with his cousin Roran, on a farm outside the village of Carvahall in Palancar Valley. Selena had left the infant Eragon with Garrow (her brother) and Marian and disappeared; during his childhood, Eragon knew little more about her, and nothing at all of his father. Eragon was fifteen years old, a year from manhood, when he discovered the strange blue stone that he soon realized was a dragon egg.

Eragon was ushered into the ancient ways of the Dragon Riders by Brom, who had been hiding in plain sight as the village storyteller. When Galbatorix's agents, the evil Ra'zac, came looking for the missing dragon egg, Eragon managed to elude them, but the Ra'zac still destroyed his home and murdered Garrow. Eragon fled Carvahall, but not before Brom insisted he was coming along. The mysterious old storyteller gave Eragon a red sword, which unbeknownst to Eragon was Zar'roc, a Dragon Rider sword. On the way to the city of Dras-Leona, Brom finally revealed he was an agent of the Varden, a resistance group fighting the Empire, and that he had been waiting for a new Dragon Rider to appear. During another Ra'zac attack, a young man named Murtagh appeared and tried to help them, but Brom was mortally wounded while protecting Eragon. As he lay dying, Brom revealed that he himself had been a Dragon Rider and that his dragon's name had been Saphira.

Eragon was later captured and imprisoned in the Empire city of Gil'ead by the Shade Durza. The elf princess Arya was also imprisoned there, but with the help of Murtagh, they all escaped. They reached the rebel Varden, who lived in secret in the dwarven land of Farthen Dûr, a hollow volcanic crater and home to the capital city of Tronjheim. The Empire soon attacked the rebel base in what history records as the Battle of Farthen Dûr. During this battle, Eragon and Saphira showed their valor, and Eragon accomplished the rare feat of killing a Shade, his former tormentor Durza, making the young Rider a Shadeslayer. The victory was not without great cost: Eragon sustained a grievous wound that greatly incapacitated him. After this, he was summoned to Ellesméra, where he and Saphira received intensive Dragon Rider training under the tutelage of the great Rider Oromis and his dragon, Glaedr. Eragon's wound was fully healed at the elf ceremony of the Agaetí Blödhren. At that point, he was also given much of the appearance, strength, and speed of an elf.

Newly healed, Eragon returned to the Varden, who were now on the brink of battle with the Empire at the Burning Plains. During the battle, the dark Rider Murtagh not only defeated Eragon and claimed Zar'roc but also told Eragon that they were brothers, sons of Selena and Morzan. Later, Oromis revealed that Brom is Eragon's real father and that Murtagh is only his half brother.

After the battle, Eragon helped rescue Sloan and his daughter, Katrina, who had been kidnapped by the Ra'zac during the siege of Carvahall. Although he and Roran rescued Katrina, Eragon concealed the fact that Sloan was alive. After seeing his cousin and Katrina safely off to the Varden, Eragon interrogated Sloan, who had betrayed his people but was himself betrayed by the Empire (with the Ra'zac plucking out his eyes during his imprisonment). Eragon finally compelled Sloan to go to Ellesméra, where he remains a captive of the elves. Afterward, Eragon fulfilled a vow to avenge Garrow's and Brom's deaths by tracking the Ra'zac to Helgrind, where he slew what he believed to be the last of its kind.

Although he has proven himself in battle, Eragon has a tender side. He had long been infatuated with Arya. At the Agaetí Blödhren he professed his love to her—and she rebuffed him. Eragon presided over one happy lovers' union, giving his blessing to the marriage of Roran and Katrina. Eragon's deepest relationship is with Saphira. They share an intimate connection: one common to Riders and dragons and which continues to deepen over time.

Eragon has become respected throughout the land, and his exploits are already the stuff of legend. He was adopted by the late king Hrothgar into his Ingeitum clan, and is a friend and confidant of the new dwarf king, Orik. Eragon has received the highest honor the elf nation can bestow upon an outsider: the ring Aren. Even the Urgals have a special name of respect for the young Rider: "Firesword." Eragon has also pledged his loyalty to Nasuada.

When Eragon found himself in need of a sword after Zar'roc was taken, he went to Rhunön for help. Rhunön—the ancient elven blacksmith and creator of all the Dragon Rider swords—had vowed never to create another, but she relented on Eragon's behalf and, with his aid, forged Brisingr, perhaps her finest achievement.

SEE BATTLE OF FARTHEN DÛR, BROM, CARVAHALL, DRAGON RIDER SWORDS, AND RORAN.

IN THE FIRST DRAFT OF BOOK ONE,
ERAGON WAS NAMED KEVIN.

KEVIN?
Christopher Paolini

ERISDAR

The flameless lanterns invented by the elves. Because Erisdar's magical quality provides a limitless and self-sustaining glow of multicolored light, the Erisdar have replaced traditional lanterns in elven and dwarven cities.

EVANDAR

The elf king and husband of Islanzadí, renowned for his wise and generous nature. In one famous incident, King Evandar lost his sword while battling Urgals but was saved when a mysterious raven swooped down and clawed out the eyes of an advancing Urgal. The grateful king blessed Blagden, the raven, with a spell that gave the bird intelligence and an extended life span.

ÉWAYËNA

This once-proud elven city was completely destroyed and its citizens slaughtered by Galbatorix and the Forsworn during the Fall of the Dragon Riders.

FADAWAR

Born of the Sagabato family, Fadawar is warlord of the Inapashunna and other tribal peoples. Fadawar competed with Nasuada for leadership of the Varden through the arduous ritual known as the Trial of the Long Knives, but he lost the bloody ordeal.

See TRIAL OF THE LONG KNIVES.

FAELNIRV

A favored alcoholic beverage of the elves brewed from crushed elderberries and spun moonbeams. More than a heady drink, faelnirv is an energy-boosting beverage that can sustain the strongest man for days.

FAIR FOLK

SEE ELVES.

FAIRTH

An image, real or imaginary, that elves fix by magic on a prepared square of polished slate. Originally designed as an alternative to portrait drawing and painting, the fairth was also used by Dragon Riders of old to test a potential Rider's powers of concentration and perception. Oromis introduced Eragon to this technique during their many training sessions. Eragon produced a fairth of Arya that portrayed her as the most beautiful woman in the world, thus revealing his romantic feelings for the elven princess.

FALBERD

SEE COUNCIL OF ELDERS.

FALL OF THE DRAGON RIDERS

The period from 7896 to 7900 AC when the noble dragons and their Riders fell before the sword of Galbatorix and the thirteen corrupted dragons and Riders of the Forsworn. The moment of Galbatorix's victory and the dawn of his Empire is fixed at the death of Vrael, the last, embattled leader of the Riders.

FANGHUR

Also known as "wind-vipers," these nearly twenty-foot-long creatures have leathery wings, serpentine bodies, and dull green and brown scales. They physically resemble dragons but have neither their intelligence nor their fire-breathing ability. They are deadly, however, and their favored method of hunting is to immobilize their prey telepathically before the kill. They are one of the five animals unique to the Beor Mountains.

FÄOLIN

A member of the elven royal guard and longtime companion of Arya, whom he met while living in Ellesméra. In order to be close to Arya, Fäolin volunteered to accompany her and the elf Glenwing as guardians of the dragon egg stolen from Galbatorix. They successfully transported the egg between the elves and Varden numerous times until they were ambushed by Durza and a band of Urgals, and Fäolin was killed in the attack.

FARICA

Nasuada's handmaiden and trusted confidante.

FARN

A dwarf warrior and member of King Orik's personal guard who often serves as Orik's trusted messenger to dwarf clan chiefs and ambassadors at the royal court.

FARR
A dwarf.

FARTHEN DÛR

This massive volcanic crater, estimated to be ten miles deep and ten miles wide, has been home to the dwarven people ever since climate change transformed their land of old into what is known today as the Hadarac Desert. Here they built the glorious city of Tronjheim, undergirded by a network of tunnels. Farthen Dûr has also served as a base for the rebel Varden and was the battleground for one of the great clashes between the Varden and the Empire.

SEE BATTLE OF FARTHEN DÛR *AND* TRONJHEIM.

FEINSTER

Situated on the southwestern coast of Alagaësia, this Empire city was governed by Lady Lorana, the descendant of four generations of rulers of this city. A wise and respected sovereign, Lady Lorana was forced to swear fealty to Galbatorix in the ancient language and did her best to defend her city from Varden forces during the Siege of Feinster. Feinster fell, and Lorana surrendered peacefully to Eragon and Arya, asking only that her subjects be treated well.

See Siege of Feinster.

FELDA

See Byrd.

FELDÛNOST

This sure-footed mountain goat, one of the five animals unique to the Beor Mountains, is not only prized by dwarves for its wool, milk, and meat but is also considered vital to the dwarves' survival in the Beors. Members of the Dûrgrimst Feldûnost are respected for tending these animals and the fields, even under the threat from Galbatorix.

See Ghastgar. *See also* Dwarf Clans *in the appendix.*

FELDÛNOST LOOK LIKE REGULAR MOUNTAIN GOATS, BUT WITH
THE HORNS OF BIGHORN SHEEP.

Mountain goat.

Bighorn sheep.

Fiolr

Elf head of House Valtharos and Naudra's mate, Lord Fiolr is keeper of the sword Támerlein. Fiolr considers the sword as precious as the very air he breathes but deems himself unworthy to wield it. Fiolr offered the dark green blade to Eragon, who had lost Zar'roc. But the instant Eragon gripped the hilt and found it too large, he knew the magnificent sword was not appropriate for him and, with apologies, declined the offer.

See Dragon Rider swords.

Firesword

See Eragon.

FIREWEED

A plant used to alleviate bad breath and indigestion in dragons. It is believed that fireweed was originally discovered by the first wild dragons, who passed the knowledge of its medicinal properties down through the generations.

FISK

A carpenter from Carvahall whose skills helped his beleaguered village's defense during a siege by the Empire. Fisk led the building of fences and construction of shields, which saved many villagers, including Roran. Fisk and his wife, Isold, were among those who escaped Carvahall's destruction, and they currently reside with the Varden's traveling army.

FISTS OF STEEL

SEE ASCÛDGAMLN.

FLETCHER

A Varden warrior.

FLINT

A sailor for Clovis the fisherman.

Floating Crystal of Eoam
See Southern Isles.

Folkvír
The horse ridden by Eragon during his Dragon Rider training in Ellesméra. Elven horses are not submissive, and humans can ride upon them only with their consent.

Formosa
See Forsworn.

Forsworn
Also known by the elves as the Wyrdfell, the Thirteen Forsworn were the True Believers during Galbatorix's rise to power. Their ranks included both elf and human Dragon Riders, all willing to throw over the legacy established by their valiant lineage.

Morzan was the first Dragon Rider seduced by Galbatorix, and his first act as a member of the Forsworn was to unlock the gates of Ilirea, making it the first city to fall to Galbatorix. As Galbatorix's power grew, a dozen more Riders and their dragons became corrupted and joined the cause. Notable members of the Forsworn included Kialandí, a female elf responsible for capturing and torturing Oromis and reportedly murdering the Rider Arva during the Siege of Ilirea, and Kialandí's comrade Formosa, who assisted in the capture and torture of Oromis.

Many of the Forsworn fell to Undbitr, the sword of Brom, including Morzan. The evil dragons were driven to madness and suicide after dragons opposing

Galbatorix cast the spell Du Namar Aurboda ("The Banishing of the Names"). Despite their own defeats and misfortune, the Forsworn were successful in establishing Galbatorix's power, and today the king controls his Empire through vast armies and magic forces.

See GALBATORIX *and* MORZAN.

FREDRIC

A human warrior and weapon master in the Varden army. Fredric has advised Eragon and prominent Varden members on appropriate weapons for any battle situation. Fredric can often be seen on the sparring field, honing his skills and sharing his knowledge with the Varden, dwarf, and Surdan warriors who eagerly join him.

FREOWIN

A dwarf.

FREWIN

See ODELE.

FRICAI ANDLÁT

See TÚNIVOR'S NECTAR.

FUNDOR

A powerful dragon of old, renowned for defeating a giant sea snake.

FURNOST

A small Empire town situated on the northern shores of Lake Tüdosten. Furnost's most celebrated resident is Hefring, a Varden spy who successfully stole one of Galbatorix's three remaining dragon eggs.

FÛTHARK

A pioneering weapon smith among the dwarves and onetime leader of the Ingeitum clan. Legend has it that Fûthark taught his craft to Rhunön, creator of the Dragon Rider swords and the greatest weapon smith of the elves.

See RHUNÖN.

GALBATORIX

The once-promising Dragon Rider whose quest for supreme power has changed the course of Alagaësian history. He was born and raised in Inzilbêth (a city that has since been destroyed). In accord with the tradition by which youngsters were presented to selected dragon eggs, he was chosen by one embryonic dragon to be its Rider. When the dragon Jarnunvösk hatched, both dragon and Rider joined the ranks of the humans and elves who were sent to Vroengard island for training. Galbatorix and Jarnunvösk excelled at their studies and showed great promise, with no hint of the darkness to come.

Upon the conclusion of their training, Galbatorix, his dragon, and some friends ventured into the dangerous Spine. It was an act of poor judgment that would alter the young Rider's life. While camping, the group was attacked by a band of Urgals, who butchered Galbatorix's friends and mortally wounded Jarnunvösk. Only Galbatorix survived, and it is said that his madness began when he found himself alone in the threatening wilderness, surrounded by the corpses of his friends and his beloved dragon.

Galbatorix returned to Vroengard, where he was brought before the ruling council of Dragon Riders to answer for the death of his dragon and companions. In addition to his poor judgment, the council saw Galbatorix's slippery hold on sanity. When Galbatorix pleaded for a new dragon, he was denied. In that instant, Galbatorix's hatred and loathing of his colleagues and all that the Dragon Riders stood for was born. From then on, he started plotting to destroy them all.

Galbatorix returned to the Spine, where he lived in seclusion and began to prepare his vengeance. He first mastered black magic sorcery, and his first victim was one of the Dragon Rider Elders, whom he killed in cold blood. He then began to destroy from within, luring other Riders to his cause. The first Rider he seduced was Morzan, who helped him steal the dragon Shruikan, whom Galbatorix bound to his will through magic spells—a blasphemous imitation of the traditional union of dragon and Rider. Along with Morzan, twelve more dragons and Riders would come to Galbatorix's side. He named his followers the Thirteen Forsworn and went to war against the Dragon Riders.

The ferocity of Galbatorix and his Thirteen Forsworn killed almost all Riders and dragons, what is known as the Fall of the Dragon Riders. When Galbatorix killed King Angrenost of the Broddrings, he declared himself king of Alagaësia.

But one hope remained—the Rider Brom. Like his fellow Rider Oromis, Brom had fought valiantly during the war but would go into hiding. Brom's blows against Galbatorix's Empire included organizing the various factions throughout Alagaësia into the cohesive rebel group known as the Varden. Brom and the Varden slew others of the Forsworn and dealt a blow to Galbatorix's dreams of a dark league of Dragon Riders by stealing one of the king's three remaining dragon eggs. It was during this time that Galbatorix's only remaining Rider, Morzan, was slain by Brom.

But Galbatorix continued to expand his power, striking out at the dwarves and elves, forcing both races into hiding. Galbatorix, through dark magic, compelled the Urgals to fight for him with the help of his lieutenant, the Shade Durza. It is believed that much of Galbatorix's power comes from the precious dragon Eldunarí (the gemlike objects within which dragons store their consciousnesses and magical energy).

However, as Galbatorix coalesced his power, so also did the forces of resistance gather their own strength. The Varden had forged an alliance with the dwarves, who gave the rebels sanctuary in their home in Farthen Dûr. Galbatorix discovered the rebel stronghold and sent Durza to lead an army of Urgals to destroy it. The Battle of Farthen Dûr marked the first stunning defeat for Galbatorix—the Urgal army was routed, Durza was slain, and the spell that bound the Urgals to the Empire was broken.

Galbatorix vowed to crush all resistance to his Empire, but ensuing struggles, including the Battle for the Burning Plains and the Siege of Feinster, were Varden victories. A key figure in the fight, who also embodied a rebirth of the Dragon Riders, was young Eragon of Carvahall, who had bonded with Saphira, the hatchling of the king's stolen dragon egg. Eragon first proved his valor at the Battle of Farthen Dûr, where he killed Durza, and has emerged as a leader of the resistance movement.

But Galbatorix is feared, and his dream of ruling all of Alagaësia remains within reach. Galbatorix is firmly in control of his Empire, which spans the western half of the continent and where he maintains his vast standing armies. Galbatorix has begun fulfilling his vision of Dragon Riders beholden to his Empire, beginning with Morzan's son, Murtagh, who with his dragon, Thorn, have been trained by Galbatorix and his enslaved dragon, Shruikan. At present, peace seems as far away as it has ever been since Galbatorix's bloody rise to power. Galbatorix seeks to capture Eragon and Saphira alive and force them to serve him. The one weakness that Eragon and Saphira have learned about Galbatorix is that his madness has left him with gaps in logic.

The names for Galbatorix include the Dragon Killer and the Dragon King. The Urgal title for him is Ushnark the Mighty. *Ushnark* means "father" in the Urgal tongue.

GÁLDHIEM
Dwarf chief of the Feldûnost clan.
SEE DWARF CLANS IN THE APPENDIX.

GALFNI
A dwarf city near the eastern edge of the Beor Mountains.

GALINA
The daughter of Clovis the fisherman.

GALTON

A grocer in Teirm.

GAMBLE

A member of the Varden in Surda.

GANNEL

Dwarf chief of the Dûrgrimst Quan. During Eragon's visit to the dwarf nation's sacred temple Celbedeil, Gannel instructed Eragon on dwarven mythology and customs. He also gifted Eragon with a necklace that would block others from scrying Eragon or Saphira as long as Eragon wears it.

SEE DWARF CLANS *IN THE APPENDIX.*

GARETH

Bartender at the Green Chestnut in Teirm.

GARROW

Brother of Selena, the son of Cadoc, husband of Marian, father of Roran, and uncle of Eragon. Garrow and Marian had raised Eragon from birth as if he were their son, but before she died, Marian revealed to Eragon that they were his aunt and uncle, not his parents. After Marian's death, Garrow moved with Roran and Eragon to an abandoned farm in Palancar Valley that lay ten miles from Carvahall, the farthest farm from the village.

Garrow had a "lean, hungry face with intense eyes" and struggled to keep himself and the two boys fed. Garrow hoped to one day pass on his farm to Eragon and Roran, and he taught them everything he knew about hunting and farming. Yet he was pleased when Roran announced that he was taking a job as a miller in Therinsford and planned to marry Katrina. During the Ra'zac's attack on Eragon, who they suspected had one of the Empire's dragon eggs, Garrow was killed and his farm was destroyed.

GARVEN

A captain of the Nighthawks, Nasuada's guards. He's a burly man with a crooked nose. When Blödhgarm arrived at the Varden, Garven was assigned to probe his mind. After the probe, Garven's spirit faded and Nasuada decided he should be removed from active duty until he recovered.

GARZHVOG

The battle-hardened Kull and leader of the Bolvek tribe of Urgals, Garzhvog— addressed with the title of respect "nar"—was instrumental in the Bolvek's decision to forge an alliance with the Varden. When he met with Nasuada, the eight-and-a-half-foot-tall ram allowed his mind to be searched to assure them of his noble intentions. Nar Garzhvog led Urgals, Kull, and Varden in battle against Galbatorix's army in the Battle of the Burning Plains and the Siege of Feinster. Afterward, the trustworthy Kull accompanied Eragon most of the way to Farthen Dûr as a protector so that Eragon could attend the dwarves' clanmeet, which was held to elect a new king.

GASHZ

A top-ranking Urgal commander in Galbatorix's Urgal army. Gashz was missing after the Urgal defeat in Farthen Dûr and is presumed dead.

GËDA'S LIGHT

The phenomenon Eragon mentions in the poem he wrote for the Agaetí Blödhren celebration.

GEDRIC

A Carvahall farmer known for his work tanning animal hides. When the Empire attacked Carvahall, Gedric joined the villagers who fled to Surda. Today he travels with the Varden army across the plains of Alagaësia. Gedric recently received a sphere of gold from Eragon, who was repaying a debt from when he stole several of Gedric's tanned hides during his own escape from Carvahall.

GEDWËY IGNASIA

"Shining palm" in the ancient language. This permanent silver mark on a Dragon Rider's palm appears after contact with a dragon hatchling and is the ultimate symbol of the bond between dragon and Rider. When working a spell, the Rider's shining palm glows with a bright white light.

GEM OF SINDRI

See Az Sindriznarrvel.

Gerand

Revered as the greatest warrior of all time and the subject of "The Song of Gerand." Although Gerand put down his sword to raise a family, a blood feud threatening his family compelled him to return to his warrior ways. It was his proclivity for killing his enemies with a simple hammer that inspired Roran to arm himself with a hammer.

Gertrude

An esteemed healer in Carvahall, Gertrude nursed Eragon back to health by tending the wounds he suffered on his first flight with his dragon, Saphira, during their escape from the Ra'zac. Gertrude escaped her village's destruction and continues her healing work with the soldiers of the Varden.

Ghastgar

A traditional dwarven contest conducted with opponents riding the backs of Feldûnost, the horned mountain goats of the Beor Mountains. One contestant is armed with a spear; the other is unarmed but carries a shield. They ride toward each other and, when the distance narrows to less than thirty feet, the javelin carrier throws his weapon at the other rider, who attempts to catch it.

Gilderien the Wise

Gilderien the Wise, an ancient elf magus and protector of Ellesméra, draws his power from the White Flame of Vándil. Gilderien has successfully defended the elves' capital city for more than two thousand years.

See Ellesméra.

GILDINTOR

A legendary steed.

GIL'EAD

This feared Empire city, situated by Isentar Lake and the Ramr River, is a center of commerce for hunters and fishermen and a major garrison for Galbatorix's army. At the center of the city is the infamous citadel that has imprisoned many enemies of the Empire, including Princess Arya and Eragon.

GIRL WITH NO NAME

See BLADESINGER.

GLAEDR

The dragon of the Rider Oromis, who initially survived the Fall of the Dragon Riders, Glaedr is a gold-colored, very large, very old dragon. When Glaedr hatched and bonded with the young elf Oromis, the pair went to the Dragon Rider island of Vroengard to begin their training. They quickly rose above their classmates and, as dragon and Rider, had years of faithful service and were known throughout Alagaësia. They had retired to a new life as teacher and mentors for a new generation of Riders when Galbatorix began his rebellion. Though Glaedr survived the Fall of the Riders, he did lose a leg in battle with the Forsworn. When Eragon and Saphira came to Ellesméra for training, Saphira became infatuated with Glaedr, but he rebuffed her and kept her focused on her training.

Glaedr experienced body death when he and Oromis emerged from hiding to battle Murtagh and Thorn in Gil'ead. He lives on through his Eldunarí but, lost in grief, has stayed silent since Oromis's death.

See Oromis and Glaedr.

Paolini once actually saw a field of yellow lichen, like the one Glaedr, Eragon, and Saphira land on in *Eldest*.

Glenwing
See Arya *and* Fäolin.

Glûmra
See Mord, Family of.

Gnaevaldrskald
Elf author of the famous autobiographical work *The Travels of Gnaevaldrskald*. A scroll of this work was part of the assigned reading Oromis gave Eragon when he and Saphira were undergoing their Dragon Rider training with the elves. The

work revealed much about the Urgals, notably that social stature was based on combat, whether raiding a village to prove valor or engaging in one-on-one combat to display one's strength to a prospective mate. Eragon would conclude that although this led to an endless cycle of violence through the generations, at least Urgals were consistent, which was more than he could say for his fellow humans.

SEE OROMIS AND GLAEDR AND URGALS.

GNOSTVIK
SEE RUNES.

GOKUKARA
The praying mantis goddess of the wandering tribes.

GOLDEN GLOBE
A tavern in Dras-Leona where Eragon and Brom once stayed.

GRASS SHIP
The little sailing ship that Arya made of blades of grass during a journey with Eragon. No more than four inches long, it was fashioned by hand in exquisite detail, including railings and benches for rowers and portholes no bigger than raspberry seeds. With a gentle breath and the ancient language word *flauga* ("fly"), the little ship set sail upon the wind. As it takes its energy from the plants below, the little ship could conceivably fly forever.

Gray Heath

A damp and barren piece of land in Empire territory, southeast of Helgrind. The dwarven name for the area is Werghadn, meaning "the ugly land."

Gray Man

See Angvard.

Graytooth

A middle-aged member of King Orrin's royal Surdan cavalry.

Green Chestnut

A tavern in Teirm.

Greta

An old woman who lived among the Varden and took care of an orphan babe. When Eragon arrived in Farthen Dûr, she begged him to bless the child.
See Elva.

Grey Folk

The race that lived on the far side of the Western Sea responsible for creating the ancient language, which they bound to the energy that is magic. The fusion of language and magic was instituted because, once upon a time, all a magician needed to cast a spell was the ability to mentally sense magic and the will to use it. But without discipline, many unplanned and chaotic enchantments were loosed upon the land. The ancient language was created to provide a structure for the use of magic. Although the Grey Folk's efforts to bring order to the use of magic has been documented, their subsequent history is a mystery. Ironically, legend holds that the Grey Folk lost their magical abilities after creating the ancient language and gradually faded away, like the ruins of an abandoned city.

SEE MAGIC.

GRIEG

An employer of the slavers who work for Torkenbrand.
SEE SLAVERY.

GRIMRR HALFPAW

King Grimrr Halfpaw is the presiding ruler of werecats during Alagaësia's second war with Galbatorix. Acting as the official speaker of his race, Grimrr met with the leaders of the resistance against Galbatorix, including delegates from the Varden, Surda, and the elves. On behalf of his race, the king agreed to form an alliance with the Varden, asking in return for the group to provide the werecats with food and provisions during the war.

Standing at nearly the same height as a mature dwarf, the aged and scar-ridden werecat radiates authority and commands respect from members of his own race as well as outsiders. The king dresses modestly for his position, choosing to wear only a loincloth and a tunic, decorated with the skulls of small game. Most notably, the werecat is missing two fingers on his left hand.

Grimrr bears a unique and mysterious string of honors and titles, which include His Most Exalted Royal Highness, King of the Werecats, Lord of the Lonely Places, Ruler of the Night Reaches, and He Who Walks Alone.

GRIMSTBORITH

In Dwarvish, the clan chief. Literally translated as "halls' chief."

GRIMSTCARVLORSS

In dwarven clan culture, *grimstcarvlorss* means "keeper of the house" or "arranger of the house." Duties include making sure clan families pay their tithes, that herds are properly grazed and stores of feed are maintained, and that everyone has what they need—women enough fabric for weaving, warriors the proper weaponry and equipment, blacksmiths enough ore. It is said that a grimstcarvlorss can make a clan—or destroy it.

GUNNAR

A sailor under Clovis the fisherman.

GÛNTERA

King of the gods for the dwarf nation. Considered a god of war and scholarship. This supernatural being has fickle moods but is appeased by burnt offerings at births and deaths, at the solstices, and before sowing season. Before battle, dwarven soldiers pray to Gûntera as he gives order to the world. (It is said he fashioned the landscape itself from the bones of a giant.)

Gûntera also manifests to give the blessing vital to the induction of a new dwarven monarch. The newly crowned Orik has told Eragon that his own legitimate rule was not assured until the god placed the helm on his head. Eragon, as an adopted member of Dûrgrimst Ingeitum, prayed to the god to still the wind that hindered his and Saphira's journey to Du Weldenvarden before the Siege of Feinster. That very night the howling wind abated.

See ORIK, KING.

HABERTH

The farrier near Therinsford from whom Brom and Eragon buy their mounts Snowfire and Cadoc.

HADARAC DESERT

The vast desert that spreads across central Alagaësia. The historic region has been home to the dwarf nation, dragons, and the wandering tribes. It was once a verdant plain, but climate change transformed the land into a desert, which forced the dwarves to relocate to the Beor Mountains. However, the hot, dry climate was perfect for the dragons, and it was there that this ancient race lived and died and collected their store of disgorged Eldunarí. A notable geographic feature is Du Fells Nángoröth, a small mountain chain in the center of the desert.

HADFALA

Dwarf chief of Dûrgrimst Ebardac.
SEE DWARF CLANS *IN THE APPENDIX.*

HAEG

The wizard hermit who saved the youth Carsaib when he was dying in the desert. After nursing him back to life, Haeg trained Carsaib in sorcery. After Haeg's death, his apprentice was consumed by spirits and transformed into the Shade Durza.

HALL OF HELZVOG

The place where dwarves devoutly wish their spirits will go upon their death.
SEE DWARVEN BURIAL RITES.

HALMAR

A Varden man.

HAMILL

A chandler in Teirm.

Hamund

A son of Loring.

Harald

A Varden man.

Hargrove

A master of telepathy and "mindbreaking," Hargrove instructed the young Nasuada on telepathic protection and defense. He had only one leg.

See MINDBREAKERS.

Harwin

A sentinel who shot at Eragon and Saphira on the Burning Plains.

Havard

Dwarf chief of Dûrgrimst Fanghur.

See Dwarf Clans *in the appendix.*

Hearth Rug

See Urgals.

HEART OF HEARTS
See ELDUNARÍ.

HEART OF STONE
See KNURLNIEN.

HEDARTH
A dwarven outpost at the mouth of the Edda River and Az Ragni. A favored supply stop for travelers, this easternmost Alagaësian town is the only dwarf settlement outside of the Beor Mountains and the closest to the elf nation.

HEDIN
One of the guards of the dwarf clan chief Ûndin.

HEFRING
A Varden spy stationed in Furnost, the small town at the northern end of Lake Tüdosten. Hefring was selected by the Varden leadership to infiltrate Galbatorix's castle and steal the three dragon eggs in his possession. Hefring stole one egg but, for unknown reasons, did not deliver it to the Varden. Both the Empire and the Varden searched for Hefring. Brom spent seven months pursuing him. However, it was Morzan who found Hefring and took the egg from him; Brom then caught up with Morzan, slew him and his dragon, and took the egg from his corpse. Hefring disappeared; his current whereabouts are unknown.

HEGRAZ
See MAGHARA.

HELEN LONGSHANKS
See JEOD.

HELGRIND

Also known as Dark Gates, this bare mountain with three soaring peaks and one small peak lies just east of Dras-Leona. An evil energy emanates from Helgrind, which is the site of a dark religion that involves self-mutilation and flesh offerings. On a full moon, gifts are brought as offerings to the gods believed to dwell there. Eragon, Saphira, and Roran discovered the secret lair of the Ra'zac that lay within the mountain's interior.

See RA'ZAC AND SLOAN.

HELGRIND WAS INSPIRED BY
SHIPROCK PEAK IN NEW MEXICO.
IT MEANS "THE GATES OF DEATH"
IN OLD NORSE.

Helzvog

The dwarven god of stone. Although Gûntera is considered king of all dwarven gods, Helzvog is the most beloved of the dwarven deities. In ancient days, when the giants who walked the earth were vanquished by the gods, Helzvog was the only god who believed the land should be peopled by a new race of beings. He therefore created the first dwarves. A volcano is known as "Helzvog's Womb"; lava is called "Helzvog's Blood."

See DWARVEN CREATION MYTH.

Heretic Kings and Queens

In dwarf history, monarchs who did not secure the god Gûntera's blessing but still insisted on assuming the throne. As King Orik has observed, "Without exception, their reigns were short and unhappy ones."

Herndall

The Urgal dams who rule their tribes.

Herran

The dwarf after whom is named an entire period of dwarven history, notably the time in which Dûrok Ornthrond carved Isidar Mithrim.

Heslant the Monk

See ARCAENA.

HIMINGLADA

The dwarf Vardrûn's daughter, Thorgerd One-eye's wife, Hvedra's mother, and Orik's cousin by law.

HLORDIS

In dwarven myth, the first woman created by Helzvog, the god of stone.

HOLCOMB

The father of Brom and husband of Nelda.

HORST

The blacksmith of Carvahall, husband of Elain, and father to Albriech and Baldor. The Horst family took in Eragon after the death of Garrow and worked closely with Roran, who led the villagers to the refuge of the Varden. Horst, a father figure to both Eragon and Roran, was the first to know about the blue "stone," in reality the egg bearing the dragon Saphira. His skills as a smith have since been put to good service with the Varden. In the formal setting of Roran and Katrina's wedding, Horst stood for the fatherless Roran.

HREIDAMAR

Dwarf chief of Dûrgrimst Urzhadn.
SEE DWARF CLANS *IN THE APPENDIX.*

Hrothgar

King of the Dûrgrimst Ingeitum, the forty-second leader of the dwarf race who guided the fortunes of his people through the bitter conflict with Galbatorix and the Empire, including the Battle of Farthen Dûr. Considered a wise and noble ruler, Hrothgar worked to mediate tensions between the clans and advance the standing of dwarves in Alagaësia. One of the king's last acts before his untimely death was beginning the restoration of the great symbol of the nation, the gigantic sculpted jewel known as Isidar Mithrim.

During the Battle of the Burning Plains, the aged ruler was killed by the dark Dragon Rider Murtagh, struck down with a magic spell that even the king's spellcasters could not deflect. The death sent shock waves throughout Alagaësia. Hrothgar's body was brought back to Farthen Dûr for a state funeral and the beloved king was laid to rest, entombed in stone alongside the forty-one kings who had gone before.

See Battle of the Burning Plains *and* Isidar Mithrim.

Hruthmund

The dwarf to whom the goddess Sindri imparted the knowledge of writing. The oldest form of Dwarvish writing is based on a rune alphabet named after Hruthmund—Hruthmundvik.

See rune.

Humans

The third race to have arrived in Alagaësia.
See Broddring Kingdom.

HÛNDFAST

A dwarf of the Ingeitum clan and a servant of King Orik. Fluent in the human and dwarven languages, Hûndfast has served as translator for many important guests, including Eragon.

HVALMAR LACKHAND

Ancient dwarf chief of Dûrgrimst Ingeitum who, over a thousand years ago, oversaw the initial excavation of Az Knurldrâthn in the Beor Mountains.

See Dwarf Clans in the appendix.

HVEDRA

A dwarf of the Ingeitum clan and wife of Orik, forty-third king of the nation. She is also the grimstcarvlorss of her clan.

Iduna

See Caretakers.

Igualda Falls

A waterfall in the northern end of Palancar Valley. At a half-mile high, it is one of the tallest waterfalls in the Spine.

See Ismira, Sloan, *and* Spine, The.

Ildrid the Beautiful

Elf and mother of Blödhgarm; aunt of Liotha.

Ília Fëon

An elven city in Du Weldenvarden. The name means "Place of Flowers."

Ilirea

The city where the wisest of the Dragon Riders taught the next generation and the location of Castle Ilirea. When the Dragon Rider Galbatorix went mad and began his war on the Riders, he induced other Riders to follow him. One of them, Morzan, left the gate to Castle Ilirea unbolted, and Galbatorix entered and stole a dragon hatchling.

After Galbatorix killed the Dragon Rider leader Vrael, Galbatorix and his Forsworn came to Ilirea and deposed King Angrenost, monarch of the Broddring Kingdom. When he took Angrenost's title and his throne—and renamed the city Urû'baen—Galbatorix truly began the Empire.

See Forsworn, Galbatorix, *and* Siege of Ilirea.

Illium

See Southern Isles.

Inapashunna

One of many wandering tribes under the leadership of Fadawar.

INDLVARN

The elven term for a Rider and dragon pair in which the dragon has suffered physical death but continues to live on in their Eldunarí.

INGOTHOLD

One of the original order of Dragon Riders. *The Chronicles of Ingothold* remains a key resource for students of Alagaësian history and the golden age of the Riders.

INGVAR

The father of the hermit Tenga.

INZILBÊTH

The province infamous as the home of Galbatorix; it no longer exists.

IORMÚNGR

The dragon who was Saphira's sire and Vervada's mate. Both Iormúngr and Vervada perished in the Fall of the Dragon Riders.

IORÛNN

Dwarf chief of Dûrgrimst Vrenshrrgn. This female leader has a sultry side and has flirted with Eragon, to his great embarrassment. Although she coveted the dwarf throne for herself, she cast the decisive clanmeet vote that elected Orik ruler.

SEE DWARF CLANS *IN THE APPENDIX*.

IRNSTAD

A powerful Dragon Rider and one of only four warriors honored as a Shade-slayer. The others are Laetrí, Eragon, and Arya.

IRWIN

Surda's current prime minister. His subjects consider him a fair and honorable man who has dedicated his life to the betterment of the nation.

ISIDAR MITHRIM

This circular star sapphire, carved with the design of a rose, is sixty feet across and adorns the heights of Tronjheim. In ancient days, the dwarves discovered the original sapphire buried in stone, deep within the Beor Mountains. Dûrok Ornthrond ("Eagle-eye") was given the daunting task of sculpting the magnificent jewel, to which he devoted the next fifty-seven years. Such was his dedication that upon completion of what had become his life's work, Dûrok died. For a race that loves gemstones, Isidar Mithrim was the paragon of beauty—Nasuada of the Varden would observe it was nothing less than "the pride of their race."

During the Battle of Farthen Dûr, Isidar Mithrim was shattered by Arya and Saphira to distract Durza, who was locked in mortal combat with Eragon. The jewel's destruction caused great unhappiness among the dwarven people. Saphira offered to help repair it if the dwarves could reassemble the thousands of fragments. The restoration effort was begun by King Hrothgar, who appointed the dwarf Skeg to oversee the collection of the pieces. Thousands of hours of labor later, the final fragment was put into place and magically repaired by Saphira in time for the coronation of the new dwarf king, Orik. Originally a dusky rose color, the repaired gem was transformed by Saphira into a richer red color with streaks of gold at the center.

SEE DÛROK ORNTHROND AND SKEG.

AN EXAMPLE OF A STAR SAPPHIRE,
WHICH HAS A STAR-SHAPED
REFLECTION ON ITS SURFACE.

ISLANZADÍ

Currently queen of the elves, Islanzadí ascended to the throne after the Fall of the Riders and the death of her husband, King Evandar. The queen, famed and feared for her own strength and cunning on the battlefield, has thus far safely led her people through the war against the Empire.

The queen has not always enjoyed the best relationship with her daughter, Arya. Their major dispute began when Arya chose to leave the elves' forest and fight alongside the Varden in their struggle against Galbatorix and the Empire. When Arya disappeared while protecting Saphira's egg, the mercurial Islanzadí became depressed and reclusive, severing all contact with the elves' allied nations. When Arya was rescued from her imprisonment in Gil'ead and finally returned to Elles-méra, her mother resumed diplomatic relations with the outside world and also reconciled with her daughter. "O my daughter, I have wronged you!" the queen proclaimed.

The queen made history by formally declaring war against Galbatorix. Her wartime engagements include leading a successful assault on the Empire city of Ceunon.

See ARYA.

ISMIRA

The wife of Sloan (owner of the butcher shop of Carvahall) and mother of Katrina. A friend to all and a caring wife and mother, Ismira died after an accidental fall while picking wildflowers atop the Igualda Falls. The tragedy hardened Sloan's heart and led to dire consequences during the Empire's siege of Carvahall.

See SLOAN.

ISOLD

See FISK.

ITHRÖ ZHÂDA

See ORTHÍAD.

JARNUNVÖSK

Galbatorix's first dragon. The death of Jarnunvösk from an Urgal arrow began Galbatorix's descent into madness and awakened the power lust that forged the Empire.

SEE Du Namar Aurboda, Galbatorix, *and* Spine, The.

JARSHA

Although too young to officially serve in the Varden government, the boy Jarsha makes himself useful as a messenger for various Varden officials.

JEOD

A wealthy merchant of Teirm, Jeod led a secret life as a Varden agent who ran a smuggling operation that supplied the Varden resistance. Sometimes called

Jeod Longshanks (though not to his face), he was a friend of Brom's for more than twenty years. The two shared many adventures, including escaping from Gil'ead and surviving an attack by Morzan and his dragon. Much later, it was Jeod who informed Roran that a new Dragon Rider had appeared in Alagaësia and that it was his cousin, Eragon. Jeod explained that it was because a dragon had hatched for Eragon that the Ra'zac first came to Palancar Valley. For a time, that grim news would harden Roran's heart against his cousin.

After Galbatorix's spies within the Varden exposed him, Jeod abandoned his mansion and business to flee with his wife to sanctuary in Surda. Helen, Jeod's wife, was born of a wealthy family and accustomed to a lavish and privileged life-style. She had been ignorant of her husband's secret work with the Varden; al-though she followed him to Surda, a spartan life with the Varden has put a strain on their marriage.

Jeod is also a renowned collector of books and scrolls. Indeed, his library in Teirm included such rare items as *Domia abr Wyrda*, the forbidden work of Heslant the Monk. "There is much you can learn from books and scrolls," Jeod told Eragon when he first traveled to Teirm with Brom, who wanted to visit his old friend. "These books are my friends, my companions. They make me laugh and cry and find meaning in life."

Although now far removed from the comforts of his library in Teirm, Jeod has put his love of books to use on behalf of the Varden. Jeod's scholarship led to his discovery of a hidden passageway into Galbatorix's castle in Urû'baen, and Na-suada has assigned him the task of poring over rare books and scrolls, searching for any other points of weakness in the ancient cities the Empire now controls.

See TEIRM.

JÖRMUNDUR

The most senior commander of the Varden and once a trusted advisor to Ajihad, Jörmundur remains a trusted warrior and is a member of the Council of Elders and a counselor to Nasuada.

KAGA

The great dwarf king who tripped on a rock and was killed by an inexperienced swordsman.

KATRINA

The copper-haired daughter of Ismira and Carvahall's butcher, Sloan. After the tragic death of her mother, Katrina was raised by her father. A childhood friendship with Roran blossomed into a love affair. The two hoped to marry, but Roran's poverty prevented him from securing Sloan's consent.

When the Empire invaded Carvahall and while the villagers were frantically working to dig a defensive trench, Roran—shaken by the turn of events—threw aside caution and proposed; Katrina accepted. As the villagers prepared to head to the Igualda Falls for safety, Katrina announced their engagement to her father, who disinherited her and then betrayed Roran to the Ra'zac. Katrina was then kidnapped and held captive within Helgrind by the Ra'zac, who had double-crossed Sloan and abducted him as well. She was rescued by Eragon, Saphira, and Roran. Eragon found Sloan alive in a cell in Helgrind but lied to Roran, telling him Sloan was dead. Roran conveyed this news to Katrina; her sadness at hearing of her father's death was tempered by her joy at seeing Roran. Shortly after they reached the Varden camp in Surda, Katrina realized she was carrying Roran's child, and with Eragon's blessing, the couple decided to hold a hurried wedding.

See Roran.

Kedar

The father of Dahwar.

Kelton

A blacksmith in Ceunon who trained Horst. Kelton is respected for his talent at the forge but despised for his bawdy manner.

Khagra

A leader of the Bolvek tribe and a member of the Nighthawks, the elite troops formed to protect Nasuada.

Kialandí

See Arva *and* Forsworn.

Kiefna Long-nose

A renowned dwarf blacksmith and member of Dûrgrimst Ingeitum. Kiefna unwittingly fashioned the dagger used in the attempted assassination of Eragon. Upset that his handiwork was used for such a dastardly purpose, Kiefna aided the investigation.

Kílf

Dwarf goddess of water. According to dwarven myth, in the primordial time after the giants were vanquished, Kílf was the only god not to create a new race of beings.

SEE DWARVEN CREATION MYTH.

Kinnell

SEE DRAGON WING.

Kirtan

An elf city at the southern border of Du Weldenvarden, southeast of the capital of Ellesméra.

Knucklebones

The dried bones, inscribed with runes, from the knuckles of a dragon. Angela the herbalist cast some knucklebones, like dice, to divine Eragon's fortune during his visit to Teirm. She also makes a passing reference, in a conversation with Nasuada, to cheating at a game of knucklebones.

KNURŁA

Dwarvish for *dwarf* and translated as "one of stone." The plural is knurlan.

KNURŁNIEN

Also known as the Heart of Stone, the Knurlnien is a sacred stone reserved for high dwarven ceremonies and oath-taking. In the oath ritual, participants make an incision on their body and wet the stone with their blood while reciting an oath in the Dwarvish language. A vow taken in this manner is considered unbreakable.

KORGAN LONGBEARD

The dwarf who discovered Farthen Dûr and founded Dûrgrimst Ingeitum. As the first king of the dwarves, Korgan Longbeard is also considered the father of the nation.

SEE DWARF CLANS *IN THE APPENDIX.*

KUASTA

A city on the western coast of Alagaësia that is isolated from the other towns and cities that dot the Spine and was the first human settlement on the continent. Modern Kuasta is said to be a haven for occult practices and is celebrated as home to the Arcaena monks, who document Alagaësian history. Kuasta was also home to Holcomb and Nelda, parents of the great Dragon Rider Brom.

See Arcaena.

Kull

The elite of the Urgal race, the Kull are bigger than the typical Urgal—an eight-foot-tall Kull is considered small. Though too heavy to ride an animal, they have a natural speed that allows them to run as fast as the swiftest steed, and their endurance allows them to do so for days, if necessary, and still be ready for battle. Nar Garzhvog is a Kull of the Bolvek tribe.

Kvîstor

The dwarf who died protecting Eragon during the assassination attempt by the Az Sweldn rak Anhûin clan when Eragon was in Farthen Dûr for the clanmeet to elect a new king.

See Mord, Family of.

LÁDIN

An elf philosopher and scientist who has dedicated his life to exploring the truth of various scientific theories. Although considered mad by many, Ládin was exonerated when he proved the existence of a vacuum and won the respect of a powerful and influential science buff, King Orrin.

SEE VACHER.

LAETRÍ

An elf warrior whose stature as a Shadeslayer puts him in the rarefied company of Irnstad, Eragon, and Arya.

LÁMARAE

A delicate elven fabric created by cross-weaving the finest wool and nettle threads.

LANG

A decorated Varden warrior renowned for his ability to take on several opponents simultaneously on the field of battle.

LANGFELD, HOUSE OF

The royal family of Surda, whose lineage includes Lady Marelda, King Larkin, King Orrin, and Thanebrand the Ring Giver.

LANGWARD

The commander of a battalion in the Empire's army whose attempt to capture Eragon and Arya resulted in death for himself and his men.

LARKIN

The late king of Surda and father of King Orrin. Larkin is believed to have been the driving force behind Surda's pact with the Varden.

See SURDA.

LARNE

Youngest son of Loring.

LAUGHING DEAD

See SOLDIERS WHO CANNOT FEEL PAIN.

LAW OF HOSPITALITY

In dwarven culture, the inviolate rule that all guests be treated with kindness and respect. A brazen violation of this code was the attempted assassination of Eragon, a guest of a clanmeet, by agents of Dûrgrimst Az Sweldn rak Anhûin. Even though that clan had sworn a blood oath against Eragon, dwarves close to Eragon had assured him that the law of hospitality would not be broken.

See ANHÛIN. *See also* DWARF CLANS *IN THE APPENDIX.*

LAY OF UMHODAN, THE

An epic of the elf race. During a sword duel in which Eragon bested his longtime tormentor Vanir, the defeated elf uttered one of the famous lines from *The Lay of Umhodan*: "How swift is your sword."

LAY OF VESTARÍ THE MARINER, THE

An epic of the elf race.

Ledwonnû

Kílf's necklace and a general term for *necklace* among the dwarf race.

Lenna

See Delwin.

Lethrblaka

When a Ra'zac matures, it sheds its exoskeleton and spreads its wings, emerging into its adult form: a Lethrblaka. The Lethrblaka can mate and continue the bloodline. A Lethrblaka's intelligence is comparable to that of a dragon. Their offspring use them as mounts. The Lethrblaka arrived in Alagaësia soon after the humans and may be what drove the humans from their own lands. During the rescue of Katrina, Saphira killed the two remaining Lethrblaka.

See Ra'zac.

An early concept sketch of a Lethrblaka by Christopher Paolini (facing page).

Łianí Vine

An elven vine bearing trumpet-shaped flowers that bloom in shades of pink and white. Found throughout Ellesméra, this flower was created by the elves through singing magic.

Liduen Kvaedhí

The elven system of writing; the name means "Poetic Script." This elegant script consists of forty-two different shapes, each representing a different sound.

LIFAEN
An elf from Ceris.

LINDEL
A Varden man.

LINNËA
See MENOA TREE.

LIOTHA
A female elf and spellcaster who resides in Du Weldenvarden. Liotha has chosen to alter her physical appearance to incorporate some of the physical attributes of a wolf, like her cousin and fellow magic wielder, Blödhgarm.

LITHGOW
One of Surda's major cities. Lithgow's proximity to Aberon and Petrøvya makes it an important center of commerce.

Lithivíra

An ancient elf city within Silverwood Forest on the eastern coast of Lake Tüdosten. Once the home of the late Dragon Rider Oromis, this city of legendary beauty has been erased by time.

Loivissa

A blue lily that grows within the borders of the Empire.

Lorana, Lady

See Feinster.

Loring

A shoemaker in Carvahall and father of Larne, Darmmen, and Hamund. Loring was a leader in the village's defense, and his children were involved as watchmen and defenders during the Empire's siege. When all was lost, he and his family joined the townspeople on the dangerous journey to Surda. Loring's alias is "Wally."

MAERZADÍ

An elf who had a premonition he would accidentally slay his own son in battle. To avoid that tragedy, Maerzadí killed himself. Arya recounted the story to Eragon as a cautionary tale to illustrate that, short of killing oneself, it's difficult to avoid the future as seen in a premonition. Although elves have developed methods of reaching into the future, they have refined them to extract specific knowledge. The only experiment elven spellcasters made in "defeating time's enigmas," as Arya put it, was a disaster: their spell to scry into the past killed all the spellcasters. "Many avenues of magic have yet to be explored," Arya cautioned Eragon. "Take care not to lose yourself among them."

SEE MAGIC.

MAGHARA

The name of a mythical female Urgal who wanted to become the mate of an Urgal who had shown his prowess by defeating twenty-seven other Urgals in wrestling matches, killing four. He had not selected a mate and wouldn't consider Maghara because of her ugliness. Maghara prayed to Rahna, goddess of Urgals, for the blessing of good looks and offered the goddess her firstborn son. Her prayer was answered, and she married and bore a son and named him Hegraz. On Hegraz's seventh birthday, Rahna appeared, demanding that Maghara fulfill her promise. Maghara battled the goddess but lost both her son and the gift of beauty. Hegraz was raised by Rahna and became one of the greatest of all Urgal warriors.

SEE RAHNA.

MAGIC

Alagaësia is a land imbued with magic. The most potent spells can literally shape the world, and their power can lie dormant for thousands of years. Rhunön used a spell to make her Dragon Rider swords never go dull or break; the singing spells of the elves make plants grow as they wish and form their very cities; the elves and dwarves employ magic to make the Erisdar lanterns glow.

Magic is a means to an end. To work their will, witches and wizards use potions and spells, while Riders use magic strengthened by their mystical bond with their dragon. Dragons have a unique, instinctual connection with magic that on occasion they channel with great power. The elves themselves are magical beings—"magic flows through their veins," Eragon once wrote—and dwarves are also known to have a vast knowledge of magic.

The ancient language provides a structure for the use of magic. It is possible to perform magic without vocalizing a spell, but this is incredibly dangerous and takes a magician of tremendous gifts. Using magic takes the same amount of energy from the user's body as it would to complete the task physically.

In a memory vision left for Eragon by Brom, the deceased Rider described magical combat as dependent on intelligence and casting a spell that an opponent does not suspect. As Brom observed: "In order to ensure victory, you have to figure out how your enemy interprets information and reacts to the world. Then you will know his weaknesses, and there you strike."

Varden leader Nasuada is uncomfortable with magic, although the Varden employ spellcasters and the command structure of the Varden has been trained in protecting their minds from the Empire's magicians. (It is also believed that espionage and intelligence, not assassination, are the major tools of such magic.) Nasuada has acknowledged to herself that at the heart of the current war is Galbatorix's abuse of magic to serve his destructive rise to power, and that magic will ultimately play a major role in bringing the corrupt king to justice.

SEE ANCIENT LANGUAGE, GREY FOLK, MINDBREAKERS, SORCERY, AND WILD MAGIC.

MAHLVIKN
SEE RUNE.

MANDEŁ
SEE BYRD.

MANI'S CAVES
SEE BEOR MOUNTAINS.

MANNDRÂTH
A dwarf.

MARELDA, LADY
Lady Marelda, of the House of Langfeld, defeated Galbatorix's troops in a battle near the city of Cithrí.

MARIAN
SEE GARROW.

MARNA
A towering mountain near Gil'ead and Isenstar Lake.

MARTLAND REDBEARD
The Earl of Thun and one of Nasuada's commanders. A dedicated and fearless warrior under whom Roran has served. After a battle against the virtually unstoppable soldiers who cannot feel pain (the laughing dead), an enemy whom Roran assumed had been killed lashed out with his sword as Martland walked across the corpse-covered battlefield, severing the commander's right hand. Despite the grievous wound, Martland kicked the sword out of the enemy soldier's hand, seized a knife in his good left hand, and killed him. Martland then insisted that his soldiers go about their tasks and pay him no concern. Martland has since retired from active combat but serves the Varden as a military strategist.

Maud

One of the shape-shifting race of werecats. Maud is also known as Quickpaw, The Dream Dancer, and The Watcher. Maud is the loyal companion of the elves and their ruler, Queen Islanzadí.

See werecats.

Melian

A small town near the southern border of the Empire and Surda, rumored to be coveted by the Varden.

Menoa tree

The largest tree in the great forest of Du Weldenvarden, the Menoa tree is gigantic enough to allow a dragon to nestle in its branches. The tree is also a sentient female being with a glacial sense of time appropriate to a tree's long life, and intimately bound up with the story of Linnëa.

Although she was young and beautiful, Linnëa's elf lover grew tired of her. When Linnëa caught him cheating on her, she killed him in a fit of passion. She escaped into the heart of Du Weldenvarden, where she used the ancient language to magically fuse her body and consciousness to the Menoa tree and has since become guardian of Du Weldenvarden.

The Menoa tree is the site of the Agaetí Blödhren, the centennial elven celebration of the ancient pact that formed the Dragon Riders. During the festivities, the tree is decorated with hundreds of multicolored lanterns, creating a rainbow effect. The celebration, performed around the gigantic tree trunk, is done with respect so as not to offend the tree.

When Eragon first met the werecat Solembum in Teirm, one of the two pieces of cryptic advice Solembum gave him was: "When . . . you need a weapon, look under the roots of the Menoa tree." Upon their second journey to Ellesméra, as Eragon was searching for a sword to replace Zar'roc, he and Saphira visited the Menoa tree and asked for her help. When the tree did not answer, Saphira breathed fire on her, and Eragon had to plead for mercy with the angry tree. She relented and said she would give him the brightsteel he sought if he agreed to give her what she wanted in return. Eragon agreed; the tree then revealed the bright-steel among her roots, but she remained silent when Eragon asked what she wanted. Her wish remains a mystery.

See Agaetí Blödhren *and* Du Weldenvarden.

The Menoa tree is a type of pine tree, though no existing pine trees are anywhere close to its size. The Menoa tree shares the height of the redwood or sequoia and the width of a baobab.

Pine.　　　　　Sequoia.　　　　　Baobab.

Merlock

A wandering trader who was asked by Eragon to appraise the strange blue stone he found during a hunting trip into the Spine. Although Merlock deduced the object was crafted by magic, he declined to purchase it. Soon thereafter, Eragon discovered that it was a dragon egg, an object rarer and more valuable than the most priceless jewel.

See Eragon *and* Saphira.

Merrybell

One of the three barges Roran and the villagers of Carvahall took from Narda.

Mindbreakers

In the war-torn world of Alagaësia, a new form of combat based on magic and telepathy has emerged. Mindbreakers use the magic of the ancient language as a martial tool and have developed telepathic techniques for breaking through mental defenses to probe and control an opponent's mind. A growing number on both the Empire and the Varden side have chosen to be mindbreakers, which has increased security concerns for all royals and diplomats and has led to increased training in guarding against telepathic attacks.

See magic.

Mírnathor

The elves' name for the desolate land southeast of Helgrind. The dwarves call it Werghadn; the humans call it Gray Heath.

Moldûn the Proud

Where the Az Ragni river flows north, separate from the Beor Mountains and rising out of the plains, is Moldûn the Proud, the towering mountain revered by dwarves.

See Beor Mountains.

Moratensis

A mythic man believed to have materialized out of a magical fountain.

Mord, Family of

An old family of dwarves within Farthen Dûr. The only known surviving member of the lineage is the widow Glûmra, who today mourns Kvîstor, the son who died protecting Eragon when an attempt on his life was made by the Az Sweldn rak Anhûin clan during the clanmeet.

Morgothal

The dwarf god of fire. In dwarven myth, it is believed that Morgothal and his beloved brother, Urûr, god of the air and heavens, brought dragons into the world.

See dwarven creation myth.

Morn

The renowned brewmaster, bartender, and co-owner (with his wife, Tara) of Seven Sheaves, a cozy tavern in the heart of Carvahall. After the Empire's siege and destruction of the village, Morn and his family joined the flight to Surda. The burden of the journey was lightened by the good cheer dispensed from the kegs of mead Morn brought along.

THE TAVERN KEEPER IN CARVAHALL, MORN, WAS NAMED AFTER A LARGE ALIEN FROM THE TV SHOW STAR TREK: DEEP SPACE NINE. THE ALIEN MORN SAT AT THE BAR ON THE SHOW, NEVER SAYING ANY-THING, AND WAS HIMSELF AN ANAGRAMMATIC TRIBUTE TO THE CHARACTER NORM FROM THE TV SHOW CHEERS.

MORNING SAGE, THE
SEE OROMIS AND GLAEDR.

MORZAN
The first of the Thirteen Forsworn and confidant of Galbatorix. He was tall and raven-haired, with one blue eye and one black, and he was missing the tip of a finger. Morzan had trained as a Rider under Oromis and was a friend of Brom before being corrupted by Galbatorix. After helping Galbatorix steal a dragon hatchling from Ilirea, Morzan became Galbatorix's disciple. They stayed in a castle forsaken by the noble Riders, and there Galbatorix taught Morzan the forbidden secrets of dark magic. By the time the instruction was over, Galbatorix's hatchling, a black dragon named Shruikan, was full-grown.

With Morzan at his side, Galbatorix began his war on the Riders, his power increasing with each one they slew. Twelve Riders, lured by Galbatorix's vision of power, joined Morzan to form the Thirteen Forsworn. Morzan brought others to the dark side, including his consort, Selena, whom he trained as his personal Black Hand. Selena gave birth to Morzan's son, Murtagh. When Murtagh was three, Morzan, in a drunken rage, threw a sword that left the child with a scar across his back. Morzan, the first Forsworn, was also the last to die, slain by Brom.

SEE BROM, FORSWORN, ILIREA, MURTAGH, *AND* SELENA.

MURTAGH

The son of Morzan and Selena, Murtagh was originally an ally of his half brother, Eragon, and the Varden. But, like his father, he would become a Dragon Rider serving the cause of Galbatorix.

Although Murtagh's lineage had aroused suspicion of his intentions, when he first met Eragon, he was a stalwart friend, saving him and Brom from the Ra'zac (though Brom ultimately died from the wounds he received in the struggle) and even helping him and Arya escape from the fortress of Gil'ead. (Only later would Eragon learn that he and Murtagh shared a mother.) Murtagh joined them on the journey to the Varden sanctuary and fought bravely at the Battle of Farthen Dûr, where his valor was motivated by a chance to show he was not his father's bad seed.

Eragon had believed that his friend had died in the tunnels of Farthen Dûr, but the traitorous spellcasters, the Twins, had captured Murtagh and took him to Galbatorix's sanctum at Urû'baen. During his incarceration, Galbatorix extracted from Murtagh all he knew about Eragon, Saphira, and the Varden. And once the dragon Thorn had hatched for Murtagh, Galbatorix seized the opportunity to have a Dragon Rider serve him and forced Murtagh and the dragon to profess their loyalty in the ancient language.

Thus bound to Galbatorix, Murtagh made his first appearance as an Empire warrior and Dragon Rider during the Battle of the Burning Plains, when victory was within the grasp of the Varden forces. The Varden victory turned to dross as the dark Rider raised his left hand and his shining palm—the Rider's gedwëy ignasia mark—and shot a magic bolt of energy that killed the dwarf king Hrothgar. Murtagh then defeated Eragon, revealed that Selena had been mother to them both, and pronounced that Morzan had been their father. (Where Murtagh received this false information is unclear.) Murtagh let Eragon live, telling him they were mirror images of each other, but he took Zar'roc, Morzan's sword, and declared, "I take my inheritance from you, brother."

Murtagh has since engaged in fierce battles with Oromis and Glaedr as well as Eragon and Saphira. Murtagh's fealty to Galbatorix is ominous, given the concerns Ajihad had once expressed to Eragon: "[Galbatorix's] cursed sorcery grows stronger each year. With another Rider at his side, he would be unstoppable."

SEE BATTLE OF THE BURNING PLAINS, GEDWËY IGNASIA, MORZAN, AND SELENA.

NAAKO

A tribesman who, with Ramusewa, attends the leader Fadawar.

NÄDINDEL

One of the main elf cities within Du Weldenvarden.
SEE DRAGON RIDER SWORDS.

NADO

Dwarf chief of the Dûrgrimst Knurlcarathn and Orik's main opponent in the election for king.
SEE DWARF CLANS *IN THE APPENDIX.*

NAEGLING

See DRAGON RIDER SWORDS.

NAGRA

A giant boar that has tusks longer than a person's forearm and a snout as wide as a person's head. The Nagra (plural Nagran) is one of the five animals unique to the Beor Mountains. These fierce creatures are hunted only by the bravest dwarves, and prized Nagra meat is reserved for banquets honoring those who have shown great courage.

NALGASK

A lip balm made of melted beeswax and hazelnut oil.

NAME SLAVES

See SLAVERY.

NAMNA

The brightly woven cloth that represents the history of Urgal families and is hung by the doorway of every Urgal hut.

Narda

A small town on the western coast of Alagaësia that is isolated from the rest of the Empire and is a center of fishing and farming. As with most towns and villages in the Spine, Narda's isolation has forced its citizens to be independent and self-sufficient. It is here that Roran commissions three barges to transport the villagers of Carvahall down the coast to Teirm.

See Spine, The.

Narheim

A consummate blend of diplomat and military strategist, Narheim serves the dwarf nation as ambassador to the Varden and acting commander of the army in King Orik's absence.

Narí

An elf from Ceris.

Nasuada

The only child of Ajihad, Nasuada succeeded him as Varden leader after his death from an Urgal ambush in the aftermath of the Battle of Farthen Dûr. During the fifteen years of Ajihad's rule, Nasuada had been part of the inner circle and trained in physical and mental combat. Although often ignored because of her youth and inexperience, Nasuada came into her own during the Battle of Farthen Dûr when she refused her father's order to evacuate with the women and children. She fought bravely and even helped coordinate the defense of the city.

After her father's death, the Varden Council of Elders nominated Nasuada to be leader, assuming that if she was elected, they could control her. Nasuada did become leader, but the council had underestimated her. With a strong will—and the backing of Eragon, Arya, and her other allies—Nasuada moved the entire Varden population to Surda and led a coalition against the Empire in the Battle of the Burning Plains, in preparation for which she even welcomed the feared and hated Urgals into her forces. Before the Siege of Feinster, and with Varden leadership hanging on the outcome, Nasuada was challenged by the warlord Fadawar to the Trial of the Long Knives. Nasuada won, but she was too weakened to lead her troops into battle. Nonetheless, the Varden ultimately took Feinster.

Nasuada has been called Lady Nightstalker by the Urgals in honor of Ajihad, who had been given the name Nightstalker because of both his ferocity in hunting Urgals in the tunnels under Farthen Dûr and the color of his skin.

See Battle of Farthen Dûr *and* Siege of Feinster.

NAUDRA

The elf lord Fiolr's mate. She received Támerlein, the sword of Arva, her brother, before he died in battle during the Siege of Ilirea.

See Arva, Siege of Ilirea, *and* Támerlein.

NEIL

A fur trader of Therinsford.

NELDA

Mother of Brom and wife of Holcomb.

NËYA

See CARETAKERS.

NÍA

See SOUTHERN ISLES.

NIDUEN

A celebrated weaver of the elven queen Islanzadí's house. Niduen made clothes for Eragon on his first visit to Ellesméra.

See ELF FAMILIES *IN THE APPENDIX.*

NIGHTHAWKS

The thirty-four human, dwarf, and Urgal warriors who make up the personal guard of Nasuada. Six (two humans, two dwarves, and two Urgals) are on duty at a given time. The guard was formed after the Battle of the Burning Plains at the insistence of Jörmundur.

See KHAGRA.

NIGHTSTALKER

See AJIHAD *AND* NASUADA.

NOLFAVRELL
See BIRGIT.

NORTH SEA
On the western coast of Alagaësia is an ocean so vast it has barely been explored. Although most of the ocean is unknown and unnamed, the waters north of the town of Narda are called the North Sea.

NUADA
One of the two lovers mentioned in the song "Du Silbena Datia." The other is Acallamh.

NUALA
An elf poetess and scholar whose celebrated work includes *Convocations*.

ODELE

A young Carvahall woman who fell in love with the youth Frewin during the exodus to Surda. Although Odele's family felt her love was an infatuation, they withdrew their criticism after the personal intervention of Roran.

ODGAR

The first dwarf created by the god Helzvog.

ODRED VALLEY

A narrow valley deep within the Beor Mountains that ends at Lake Fernoth-mérna, near Farthen Dûr. The Odred Valley is favored by travelers as the safest route out of the range.

OLD ONE
See UNULUKUNA.

ORIK, KING

King Orik, son of Thrisk, nephew and adopted son of King Hrothgar, leader of Dûrgrimst Ingeitum, and forty-third dwarf king.

Because Orik had a notoriously wild youth, he spent many days in Az Knurl-drâthn to atone for his bad behavior. Before reaching adulthood, his parents passed, but he was adopted by his uncle, King Hrothgar. Young Orik not only received a behind-the-scenes education in political intrigues and affairs of state but also became an unofficial advisor to his uncle and ambassador to the Varden.

When Eragon and Saphira visited the Varden in Farthen Dûr, Orik was assigned by Ajihad to be their guide during their stay. The three quickly became friends, and when Eragon and Saphira left for Dragon Rider training among the elves at Du Weldenvarden, Orik accompanied them. Orik was not only the de facto dwarf ambassador to the elves, but also among the few of the non-elven races allowed within the sacred forest and the first dwarf in nearly a century to meet with elven royalty. (He is also believed to be the only dwarf ever to have ridden on the back of a dragon.) Orik would become the leading advocate for Eragon and the lineage of Dragon Riders among his people.

After the training at Du Weldenvarden, Orik accompanied Eragon and Saphira to Surda. There they joined the Varden army and the dwarven soldiers led by Hrothgar in the second great engagement against Galbatorix and the Empire. In that battle, Hrothgar was slain by the dark Dragon Rider Murtagh.

When Orik returned to Farthen Dûr, he saw that his uncle was laid to rest among the past kings. He became leader of his clan and, after a fierce political struggle at the clanmeet, was elected king. During this eventful time, Orik managed to marry his longtime companion, the beautiful Hvedra of the Ingeitum clan.

See BATTLE OF THE BURNING PLAINS *and* DWARVES.

Orm Blood-axe

The father of the dwarf clan chief Gannel.

Oromis and Glaedr

The last Rider and dragon to survive the Fall of the Riders. Oromis and his dragon, Glaedr, had been exceptional students when they trained in the Dragon Rider capital on the island of Vroengard and were exemplary guardians of peace and justice. After years of faithful service, they became teachers, training many apprentice dragons and Riders. When Galbatorix began his bloody quest for power, Oromis and Glaedr returned to duty and fought in many of the ensuing battles.

At one point, Oromis was captured and tortured by Galbatorix's Forsworn, escaping only after being mentally crippled and stripped of most of his magical powers. His ensuing seizures earned him the name Togira Ikonoka, "The Cripple Who Is Whole." He is also called Osthato Chetowä ("The Mourning Sage"). Glaedr, too, sustained heavy wounds and the loss of one leg. The pair realized that for the survival of their lineage, they had to go into hiding and try to stay alive so that if a dragon egg hatched, they would be able to train the new Rider.

Oromis and Glaedr lived among the elves for a century in Du Weldenvarden. Their hope for a return to past glory was rewarded as they trained and advised Eragon and Saphira. A sometimes stern taskmaster, Oromis was a careful teacher: he showed Eragon how to open his mind to the forest around him, trained him in the art of magically transporting objects over great distances, and taught him swordsmanship. Eragon, while already a skillful swordsman, was in awe of Oromis, whose body had all the innate elven qualities of speed and strength and whose very blood seemed suffused with magic. It was during his second visit to Du Weldenvarden, before the Siege of Feinster, that Eragon learned from Oromis and Glaedr the secrets of his past, with the dragon revealing that Brom—not Morzan—was Eragon's father.

While Eragon was fighting with the Varden at Feinster, Oromis and Glaedr encountered Murtagh and Thorn at Gil'ead. In the midst of the battle between the two Riders and dragons, an "unseen force" propelled them all high into the air, and Galbatorix spoke through Murtagh, using his wiles and his magic against Oromis and Glaedr. Oromis suffered a seizure, lost his sword Naegling, and then was struck a fatal blow. Glaedr's physical body was slain by Thorn, but Glaedr lives on through his Eldunarí, which was entrusted to Eragon and Saphira before the Siege of Feinster.

SEE CRAGS OF TEL'NAEÍR AND GLAEDR.

ORRIN

King of Surda, son of King Larkin, of the House of Langfeld. While King Orrin lives a spartan life befitting a wartime ruler, his one indulgence is the scientific laboratory he maintains in Borromeo Castle. He is a childhood friend of Nasuada, although there have been power struggles and differences between the king and the Varden leader.

SEE VACHER.

ORTHÍAD

Situated near the western edge of the Beor Mountains, Orthíad was once the greatest dwarf city. During the construction of Tronjheim, Orthíad became the temporary capital of the nation. The city was abandoned upon completion of Tronjheim, and the Urgals took shelter there prior to their attack on the Varden during the Battle of Farthen Dûr. The Urgals and Galbatorix refer to Orthíad as Ithrö Zhâda.

SEE TRONJHEIM.

OSILON

This westernmost elf city in Du Weldenvarden is the hub of an agricultural area that is the proverbial breadbasket for much of the elf nation. It was near this city that Arya and her royal guard were bearing the dragon egg when they were ambushed by Durza and his Urgals.

SEE ARYA.

Osthato Chetowä

See Oromis and Glaedr.

Othmund

A member of the Varden sentenced to death and executed for betraying the recent alliance between Varden and Urgals.

Otvek

A warrior of the Urgal tribe and one of three Urgals who submitted to a mind search when the tribe pledged its allegiance to the Varden. Otvek continues to fight alongside the Varden.

PALANCAR

The pioneering leader of the first humans to settle in Alagaësia. King Palancar began his reign in the valley that would bear his name—Palancar Valley. He was a wise and noble ruler for a time, but he violated his own peace pact with the elves and initiated a disastrous unprovoked war for control of the region between the Spine and Du Weldenvarden. Some believe this rash act was precipitated by the early stages of madness. King Palancar was eventually overthrown by his nobles, who had been against the war and signed a secret treaty with the elves; the king was banished as a condition of the truce, but he refused to leave the valley. The elves then constructed the tower of Ristvak'baen to keep watch over the deposed king. Palancar was killed by one of his sons, and a family legacy of assassination and betrayal ensued.

SEE BRODDRING KINGDOM.

PAOLINI NAMED PALANCAR VALLEY AFTER THE ARTIST JOHN JUDE PALENCAR, THOUGH HE DID ALTER ONE VOWEL. LATER, PALENCAR WOULD BECOME THE JACKET ARTIST FOR THE INHERITANCE CYCLE.

PALANCAR PIRATES

The name given the Carvahall villagers who, after the siege of their village, sailed by barge and ship via the southern Great Sea to the haven of the Varden. The "pirates" moniker is apt—the villagers stole the vessels they needed, aided by sailors from Narda and Teirm.

PALANCAR VALLEY

A large valley in northern Alagaësia along the Spine. It was here that the first human immigrants settled, and it is named for their leader, King Palancar. The valley's towns and villages include Carvahall and Therinsford, and natural wonders include the Anora River, which runs from the base of half-mile-high Igualda Falls, through the valley, and onto the plains beyond. At the mouth of the valley is Utgard, once a Dragon Rider watchtower. It was in Palancar Valley that Eragon, future Dragon Rider and Shadeslayer, was born.

See UTGARD MOUNTAIN.

PARLIM

See SOUTHERN ISLES.

PETRØVYA

One of several Surdan cities along the independent nation's northern border. It's a major trade city, whose commerce includes the smuggling of war supplies between Surda and the Empire.

QUIMBY
See BIRGIT.

QUOTH MERRINSSON
The son of Merrin and a talented dwarf chef who feeds Varden and dwarven troops. At one war camp, Eragon personally visited the cook to see if he could provide a meal of livestock and a barrel of mead for Saphira. Quoth is intimidated by Saphira's gargantuan appetite.

Rahna

Goddess of the Urgals, referred to as "mother of us all," hailed as the inventor of weaving and farming. It is said that in primordial days, when fleeing a great dragon, Rahna raised the mighty Beor Mountains. Also known by the title She of the Gilded Horns.

See Maghara.

Ramusewa

A tribesman who, with Naako, attends the leader Fadawar.

Ra'zac

The Ra'zac are the size of men but have the physical characteristics of insects and are considered the most evil race in Alagaësia. It is believed the Ra'zac not only followed the first humans who migrated to Alagaësia but were the reason humans fled their native land. As the elven Rider Oromis once said of them to Eragon: "They are the monsters in the dark, the dripping nightmares that haunt your race." Following the Fall of the Riders, the Ra'zac made an alliance with Galbatorix and served as assassins for the dark king. Two Ra'zac were the agents who first came to Carvahall in search of the dragon egg that the elf princess Arya had magically transported and that had been discovered by young Eragon. The creatures killed Eragon's uncle, Garrow; it was to avenge his uncle's death that Eragon left Palancar Valley with Brom. And it was the Ra'zac who killed Brom, furthering Eragon's desire to pursue and eliminate them.

A Ra'zac has a beak and fist-sized black eyes; its breath is foul, its back is humped. The Ra'zac keep themselves cloaked when among humans. Ra'zac are in a pupal state until, on the first full moon of their twentieth year, they burst out of their exoskeleton as winged creatures ready to feed on any living being. The mature creatures are called Lethrblaka and have an intelligence far superior to that of their offspring; Oromis has likened their intelligence to that of a "cruel, vicious, and twisted dragon." The Lethrblaka serve as mounts for their offspring. When Ra'zac first began haunting the land, the elves attempted to eradicate them and were nearly successful, but two Lethrblaka escaped with their pupae to continue the species.

Ra'zac cannot harness the ancient language and thus are unable to practice magic, although they can block a spellcaster's mental attacks. Because of their sensitivity to light, they favor fighting at night and do so in packs, using stealth to gain an advantage. They track by scent and can see through the darkness of a cloudy night, but they fear water, as they cannot swim. It is dangerous to come within a few feet of a Ra'zac, for its poisonous breath will stun and immobilize its potential victim.

Their numbers dwindled until only two Ra'zac (plus two Lethrblaka) lived within a hidden series of tunnels and chambers at Helgrind. Now, following the battle in which Eragon fulfilled his vow to take revenge against the creatures, they are believed to be extinct. Before the last Ra'zac died, however, it cryptically told Eragon that Galbatorix had almost "found the *name*." It also cursed Eragon, saying, "May you leave Alagaësia and never return," echoing Angela's fortune-telling in Teirm.

See LETHRBLAKA.

THE RA'ZAC ARE BASED ON JERUSALEM CRICKETS.

REAVSTONE

The southernmost coastal city of Surda and a major port. Reavstone is also another key entry point for goods smuggled between the Varden and the Empire.

RED BOAR

One of the three barges that Roran and the villagers of Carvahall took from Narda.

RHUNÖN

The greatest smith of the elves, said to have been taught the ancient art by the fabled Fûthark. Rhunön forged all the Dragon Rider swords that exist today using brightsteel, a metal smelted from ore extracted from fragments of a falling star. Upon the Fall of the Riders, Rhunön swore an oath to never craft another Rider sword. Even Brom, who had lost his original sword and was forced to use Zar'roc, begged for a new sword, but Rhunön stuck to her vow. Also, she had run out of brightsteel. For Eragon, who with Saphira collected brightsteel from the roots of the Menoa tree, she relented, circumventing her oath by guiding Eragon's hands from within his mind so that technically he was the creator of the great blue sword—Brisingr.

RIMGAR

A series of elven exercise techniques, also known as the Dance of Snake and Crane, involving stretching into and maintaining strenuous positions. Originally conceived for elven Dragon Riders, Rimgar has since become the favored exercise program for all elves.

THE RIMGAR IS SIMILAR TO A SEQUENCE OF YOGA ASANAS (POSES).

Rimmar

The dwarf responsible for leading the investigation into the attempted assassination of Eragon that occurred during his meeting with the dwarves' new king. Rimmar and his team eventually implicated Grimstborith Vermûnd in both the assassination attempt and the death of Kvîstor.

Risthart

The governor of Teirm and resident of that city's great citadel. It is believed that Lord Rishart swore fealty to Galbatorix in the ancient language and that he personally orchestrated the mysterious attacks on trading ships suspected of supplying the Varden.

Ristvak'baen

See Utgard Mountain.

Rock of Kuthian

A mysterious landmark, mentioned in the werecat Solembum's advice to Eragon in Teirm.

Rolf

Jeod Longshanks's butler.

RORAN

The son of Garrow and Marian, cousin of Eragon, and husband of Katrina. When Roran was two, Garrow and Marian adopted Garrow's nephew Eragon, the son of Brom and Selena, and raised him like a son, whereby he became like a brother to Roran. After Marian's death, Roran lived with Garrow and Eragon on a farm ten miles from Carvahall in Palancar Valley. Upon falling in love with Katrina, Roran left home to become a miller's apprentice in Therinsford so that he could have a trade and marry. Thus, he was away when the Ra'zac killed Garrow and ravaged the farm and when Eragon left Palancar Valley. Brom sent word to Roran, though, and Roran returned to Carvahall, living with Horst and Elain.

When Carvahall came under siege from the Empire, Roran emerged as leader of the refugees during the escape to refuge with the Varden. Roran, inspired by the legendary warrior Gerand, took as his weapon of choice a hammer, which earned Roran the name of Stronghammer. It was with his hammer that Roran slew the traitorous Twins during the Battle of the Burning Plains. It was just before that battle that Roran arrived on the Jiet River in the ship *Dragon Wing*, bearing Jeod Longshanks and others. Though Roran was embittered after having learned from Jeod that Garrow's death was precipitated by the Empire's desire to capture his cousin, Eragon, the two met and Roran forgave Eragon. Eragon then vowed to help Roran rescue his true love, Katrina.

Katrina was captured by the Ra'zac during the Empire's siege of the village after Katrina's father, Sloan—angry about Roran and Katrina's decision to marry against his will—betrayed Roran to the Ra'zac. Roran, Eragon, and Saphira rescued Katrina from Helgrind and the clutches of the Ra'zac after the Battle of the Burning Plains. Eragon discovered Sloan alive in Helgrind but lied to Roran, telling him Sloan was dead; Roran, believing Eragon, conveyed the news to Katrina. Katrina was pregnant with Roran's child and, once the two were safely in the Varden's camp in Surda following the Battle of the Burning Plains, a hurried wedding was arranged. Eragon blessed the bride and groom.

Roran has served under such able Varden commanders as Martland Redbeard. During this time, he had an unnerving encounter with Galbatorix's seemingly deathless enchanted soldiers, battering them with his hammer until their faces were nothing but pulp even as they kept advancing, streaming blood and emitting their ghoulish giggles. He also saw Redbeard lose his hand to the sword of one of the enchanted soldiers.

Roran defied the command of Varden captain Edric, who had ordered what Roran felt was a virtual suicide mission. On his own terms, Roran led eighty-one warriors who chose to stand with him into battle and only lost nine men, while Edric had already lost some hundred and fifty men before he was rescued. Despite being vindicated—even Nasuada admitted that if Roran hadn't defied Edric's command, no one might have survived—he had disobeyed an order from a commanding officer. As discipline was vital to maintain order, Nasuada regretfully ordered he receive fifty lashes, which Roran stoically accepted—the thought of Katrina and their unborn child bolstered Roran's spirit in the midst of his ordeal. The Varden leader ordered Angela the herbalist and the sorceress Trianna to use their powers to heal his wounds in time to lead the Siege of Feinster.

Although a natural leader, Roran has made enemies and has had his leadership contested. Carvahall villager Birgit blamed him for the death of her husband and vowed revenge. When leading a war party of Bolvek Urgals, Roran was challenged to hand-to-hand combat by the Urgal Yarbog, but Roran used his strength and wits to defeat the Urgal and retain command.

See Gerand, Katrina, Martland Redbeard, *and* Soldiers Who Cannot Feel Pain.

RUNE

A character serving as a letter in an alphabet. The Dwarvish alphabet is composed of runes, and they have three such methods of writing. The oldest is called both Hruthmundvik, after Hruthmund, whom the goddess Sindri gave the knowledge of writing, and Gnostvik, after the first five letters of the alphabet. While the old alphabet is suited to chisels, Thrangvik, the second mode of writing, is a "soft" variation of Hruthmundvik that is designed for brushes and quills. The third system, Mahlvikn, contains the secret letters that compose virtually a second language. It is used by the Quan clan for writing the holy texts of the race.

SEE DWARF CLANS *IN THE APPENDIX.*

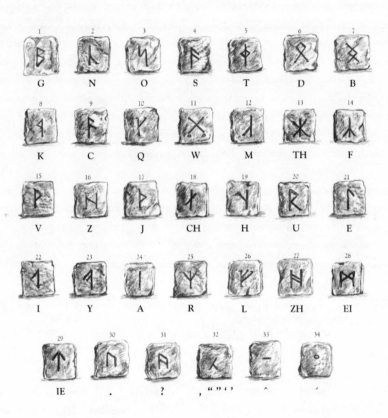

RUNES

An elf game. The dwarf Orik enjoys playing Runes in Ellesméra.

RUNNERS-OF-THE-TUNNELS

A rough translation of a Dwarvish word for those who regularly inspect the ancient tunnels of Farthen Dûr and the Beor Mountains, looking for cave-ins or other disturbances.

SABRAE

See COUNCIL OF ELDERS.

SAGABATO

A family of the wandering tribe into which the warlord Fadawar was born.

SAND

A Varden warrior.

SAPHIRA

The dragon who hatched under the watchful eye of Eragon. Her sire was Iormúngr and her dam Vervada. Saphira's egg, one of the three known dragon eggs in existence, was in the possession of the elf princess Arya when the Shade Durza and his Urgal agents almost recaptured it in an ambush. Arya succeeded in magically transporting the precious egg to a wild area of the Spine, where Eragon, alone on a hunting expedition, discovered it. Eragon had trouble naming his blue-scaled dragon until he realized that the hatchling was female; as he went through the names the storyteller Brom suggested, the dragon herself indicated her name: Saphira.

As with all dragons and Riders, Saphira and Eragon communicate telepathically and their bond is a deep and everlasting one. Saphira carries the wisdom of her race, and Eragon often turns to her for guidance and comfort.

Saphira and Eragon, along with Brom, left Carvahall to seek out the Varden, learning from the old storyteller along the way. When he perished at the hands of the Ra'zac, Saphira used magic to create a diamond tomb for Brom. Eragon later learned that before Brom died, he had entrusted Saphira with the secret of Eragon's parentage.

Together, the dragon and Rider have played a major role in all of the recent great battles against the Empire—the Battle of Farthen Dûr, the Battle of the Burning Plains, and the Siege of Feinster. During the Battle of Farthen Dûr, the revered Isidar Mithrim jewel of Trojheim was shattered by Saphira and the elven princess Arya to distract Durza, who was locked in mortal combat with Eragon. A painstaking restoration effort ended when the thousands of shattered fragments were collected, pieced together by the dwarves, and magically repaired by Saphira.

When Eragon and Saphira first arrived in Ellesméra for formal training, the dragon Glaedr took charge of the young blue dragon. Saphira became infatuated with Glaedr during their training together, but the older dragon rebuffed her and firmly kept her focused on the more important tasks at hand. Glaedr's Rider, Oromis, said of Saphira, "I've rarely seen a dragon so naturally suited to the sky."

After the Varden's victory on the Burning Plains, Eragon and Saphira undertook a rescue mission of Katrina with Roran. They confronted the Ra'zac at Helgrind, where Katrina was being held, and Saphira killed both Lethrblaka.

Eragon and Saphira sometimes faced painful periods of separation, such as when Eragon had to attend the dwarf clanmeet in Farthen Dûr.

Saphira is known by the ancient language title Bjartskular (which means "Brightscales") and the Urgal name Flametongue.

One time, Saphira, sensing Eragon's unease and uncertainty about the future, shared her own dark premonitions and hopes: *The world is stretched thin, Eragon. Soon it will snap and madness will burst forth. What you feel is what we dragons feel and what the elves feel—the inexorable march of grim fate as the end of our age approaches. Weep for those who will die in the chaos that shall consume Alagaësia. And hope that we may win a brighter future by the strength of your sword and shield and my fangs and talons.*

SEE BROM *AND* DRAGONS.

THE NAME SAPHIRA IS A PLAY ON *SAPPHIRE*.

SAPHIRA'S BLUE-TINTED VISION WAS INSPIRED BY PAOLINI'S OWN COLOR BLINDNESS.

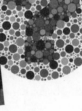

SCRYING

The magical act of conjuring up an image of a person, place, or thing by speaking the ancient language over a pool of water, a mirror, or other reflective surface. As with most magic, there are rules and limits to what a spellcaster can do when scrying. If the caster has never before encountered the desired person, place, or thing, he or she will be unable to successfully conjure the image. Also, if the caster has encountered the target but does not know the surroundings, only the target will become visible. Eragon, for some unknown reason, was able to scry the elf princess Arya, imprisoned in Gil'ead, after having seen her only in a dream and without knowing who she was.

See SEEING GLASS.

SEEING GLASS

A magical device created by the elves to enhance a magician's scrying powers and enable communication between two scrying pools.

SEFTON

A Varden swordsman wounded during the Battle of the Burning Plains.

SEITHR

The Seithr plant is endemic to a small island off the northwestern coast of Alagaësia and highly prized by jewelers for the oil extracted from its petals, which is a natural preservative for pearls. Seithr oil is rare, given the perilous waters of the North Sea that must be crossed in order to obtain the plant. A blood sacrifice

plus certain spoken words can transform the protective oil into a
noxious acidlike substance that can eat away flesh while leaving
everything else untouched. Torturers and assassins particularly
favor Seithr oil.

SELENA

The mother of Eragon and Murtagh, sister of Garrow, daughter of Cadoc,
consort of Morzan, and lover of Brom. Selena met Morzan, her first love, and
became his devoted—some would say slavish—companion, his personal Black
Hand. Morzan trained her in dark magic, armed combat, and mental defense
against psychic attack. In her first test, she used only a healing spell and a knife
to dispatch twelve warriors, slitting their throats in the process. Selena became
such an effective servant that Morzan's enemies in the Forsworn sought to use her
against him.

When Selena became pregnant, Morzan hid her within the castle, where she
gave birth to Murtagh. The baby was spirited away and raised by a nurse. Selena
witnessed Morzan's cruel treatment of her son, which led to their estrangement.
After meeting the Dragon Rider Brom, Selena changed from her dark ways and
the two fell in love. Thus began Morzan's downfall and his ultimate death at the
hands of Brom. It is said Morzan's fatal error was believing Selena would always
remain in his power. Apologists for Selena assert she had been blinded to her
husband's true nature. Brom once described her to Eragon as "full of dignity and
pride" and added: "She always helped the poor and less fortunate, no matter what
her situation." She became an invaluable Varden informant, supplying inside
information on Galbatorix, Morzan, and the Empire. Although Brom and Selena
never married, they were a devoted couple and considered themselves spiritually
bound as husband and wife. When she found herself pregnant with Brom's child,
she returned to Carvahall and lived there for five months until the baby, whom

she named Eragon, was born. She then disappeared the next day. Eragon, on his second visit to Ellesméra, learned from Oromis that Selena returned to Gil'ead, but the journey left her ill, and she died before she could be reunited with Brom.

See Brom, Garrow, Morzan, *and* Murtagh.

Serpent

A playing piece in the elves' Runes game.

Seven Sheaves

A tavern in Carvahall.
See Morn.

Shade

A sorcerer who becomes possessed by the spirits he or she has conjured.
See Durza *and* sorcery.

Shadeslayer

The title given to anyone who manages the rare feat of killing a Shade.
See Arya, Eragon, Irnstad, *and* Laetrí.

Sharktooth Island

A small island off the western coast of Alagaësia and southwest of the port city of Teirm. Its name is inspired by its shape.

She of the Gilded Horns

See Rahna.

Shrrg

One of the five animals unique to the Beor Mountains (plural Shrrgn). These gigantic wolves have razor-sharp fangs and claws.

THE SHRRG IS BASED ON THE TIMBER WOLF. CHRISTOPHER INVENTED THE WORD AFTER THINKING ABOUT THE SOUND OF A DOG'S GROWL.

Shrrgnien

One of the guards for the dwarf clan chief Ûndin.

Shruikan

The dragon that hatched from the egg that Galbatorix stole from Castle Ilirea to replace Jarnunvösk, whom he lost when the dragon was pierced through the heart by an Urgal's arrow.

See dragons, Du Namar Aurboda, Galbatorix, *and* Ilirea.

Shur'tugal

The elves' name for the Dragon Riders.

Siege of Feinster

The Varden leader Nasuada, weakened by the arduous Trial of the Long Knives, asked Eragon to lead the attack against the coastal city of Feinster, an Empire stronghold considered pivotal to their cause. (Once the Varden took Feinster, they could march on the cities of Belatona and Dras-Leona and from there attack Galbatorix's stronghold of Urû'baen.) It was also a key battle, as the alliance of Varden and Urgals was fraying and Nasuada wanted to keep the coalition together. Although Nasuada wanted Eragon and Saphira to lead the fight, believing the appearance of a dragon and Rider would cause their opponents to lose heart, Eragon felt that to defeat Galbatorix, Saphira and he needed more training from Oromis and Glaedr in faraway Ellesméra. It was a risk to let the dragon and Rider go, as Lady Lorana, ruler of Feinster, was already sending war parties out to harass the Varden troops. If Eragon and Saphira did not return in time, the Varden would have to go to battle without them. But Nasuada agreed to delay their attack. In the meantime, she placed Roran, who had just suffered the lash for his insubordination under Captain Edric, in command of a combined group of humans and Urgals in order to maintain the Urgals as allies.

The attack on the city was under way when Eragon and Saphira returned from Ellesméra and an eventful visit with Rhunön, who had worked through Eragon to forge his mighty sword, Brisingr. Saphira announced their arrival with a shattering roar and a burst of blue fire, and immediately helped Arya, who had scaled the walls of the embattled city. The first to fall to Brisingr was the captain of the soldiers guarding the city gates, who had leveled a serious curse on Eragon: "May you leave Alagaësia and never return." This was the same curse that the last Ra'zac gave just before Eragon killed it. Thereupon, the gates were opened and the Varden coalition fought their way through the city, not reaching the western end until the following dawn.

Victory was theirs by the time they reached Lady Lorana and received her surrender. But there was one last obstacle to overcome, perhaps the most dangerous of all. With Galbatorix having failed to send reinforcements, three magicians of Feinster, who had sworn allegiance to the evil king, created a Shade, Varaug. During a ferocious battle, Arya killed Varaug with the help of Eragon, making the elven royal a Shadeslayer.

SIEGE OF ILIREA

When the ancient city of Ilirea fell to Galbatorix, the Empire truly began. Ilirea had been given to the humans by the elves after the end of the war that Palancar had foolishly initiated. The city, renowned as a center of Dragon Rider training, made it an obvious target of Galbatorix's campaign. But it was also the seat of power for the Broddring Kingdom. Galbatorix and his Thirteen Forsworn laid siege to the city, captured it, and deposed King Angrenost.

SEE ARVA AND SURDA.

SÍLTHRIM

Situated deep within Du Weldenvarden, this elven city on the western shore of Lake Ardwen is considered second only to the capital of Ellesméra in greatness.

SILVERWOOD FOREST

A peaceful forest on the shores of Lake Tüdosten. In this idyllic place, the Dragon Rider Oromis was born.

SEE OROMIS AND GLAEDR.

SINDRI

Dwarven goddess of earth who brought forth human beings to populate the land after the giants who ruled the earth were vanquished.

SKEG

A talented dwarf jewel crafter and architect of the Gedthrall clan. Skeg was assigned by King Hrothgar to oversee reassembly of the shattered Isidar Mithrim. Although Hrothgar would not live to see it, after thousands of hours of piecing together the fragments, Saphira magically repaired the great jewel sculpture in time for the coronation of the new king, Orik.

SKGAHGREZH

The blood brother of Nar Garzhvog and rightful ruler of the Bolvek tribe, Skgahgrezh assumed control over Urgal forces within the Varden when his brother was escorting Eragon to the dwarves.

See GARZHVOG.

SKILNA BRAGH

A deadly poison favored by the Empire's assassins.

See TÚNIVOR'S NECTAR.

SLAVERY

Slavery came to Alagaësia with the arrival of humans. The dismal trade continues to this day in Dras-Leona and other Empire cities that boast thriving slave markets. Indeed, slavery is part of the imperial culture. There are even so-called name slaves, subjects who have been forced to swear fealty to Galbatorix in the ancient language, an oath that has been taken by most of the Empire's soldiers.

During a trek along the eastern border of the Hadarac Desert, Eragon, Saphira, and Murtagh encountered a band of slaves led by Torkenbrand. Because of this fateful encounter, Eragon vowed to free all slaves and abolish slavery forever.

SLOAN

The son of Alden and owner of the butcher shop in Carvahall, Sloan was forced to raise his daughter, Katrina, alone when his beloved wife, Ismira, died in an accidental fall off Igualda Falls. Although a loving parent, Sloan maintained a simmering rage at his loss. He was so obsessed with protecting his daughter—and so distraught that she intended to marry Roran without his consent—that during the siege of Carvahall, he betrayed his townspeople in exchange for the Empire guaranteeing Katrina's safety. Sloan ambushed and murdered Byrd, a villager serving as a watchman during the siege. But Sloan was double-crossed: the Ra'zac kidnapped him and Katrina, imprisoned them within Helgrind, and plucked out Sloan's eyes. In his and Roran's rescue of Katrina, Eragon found Sloan alive. However, he told Roran that Sloan was dead (and Roran told Katrina). After seeing Katrina safely on her way to the Varden with Roran (and ordering Saphira to go with them), Eragon returned to Helgrind alone, killed the last Ra'zac, and carried Sloan out of their lair. In trying to determine what to do with Sloan, Eragon searched the butcher's mind and found his true name. Eragon then punished Sloan by decreeing that Sloan would never again meet Katrina and compelling him to travel to Ellesméra and remain in a benign captivity with the elves.

SNOWFIRE

The horse Brom bought for himself from Haberth near Therinsford as he and Eragon set out from Carvahall in search of the Ra'zac. After Brom's death, Snowfire passed to Eragon, who in turn gave the great horse to Roran.

SOLDIERS WHO CANNOT FEEL PAIN

After the Empire's crushing defeat by the Varden at the Battle of the Burning Plains, Galbatorix asked for volunteers to undergo a spell that would render them incapable of feeling pain and thus fearless in battle, promising security for their families in return.

In their first meeting on an open plain, the Varden had a thousand soldiers against three hundred of Galbatorix's men. Not realizing that the soldiers were enchanted, the Varden soldiers lost their nerve when severely wounded men kept advancing—and laughing—despite wounds that should have disabled them. The obscene spectacle ended when King Orrin chopped off a soldier's head, proving they could be stopped for certain if beheaded. Although the three hundred were slain, it was at such a cost to the Varden that Nasuada pronounced the engagement "a grievous defeat."

Roran, on his raiding mission with Martland Redbeard, encountered a band of these soldiers camped near a nameless river. Though Martland and Roran drove the soldiers into the water and finally defeated them, the soldiers' laughter in the face of mortal wounds was unsettling. The enchanted warriors are also known as the laughing dead.

See Battle of the Burning Plains.

Solembum

The mysterious werecat companion of Angela the herbalist. Although Solembum has been known to take the form of a young male human, he usually appears as a big cat, similar to a caracal (see page 206), with golden eyes and dark fur. The witty but acerbic Solembum took a rare liking to Eragon and Saphira when he met them in Teirm. Solembum has even been seen napping on Saphira's neck. Solembum has the power to foretell the future, and has already made two prophecies to Eragon, one of which—about looking under the roots of the Menoa tree when in need of a weapon—has come true. The other—"when all seems lost and your power is insufficient, go to the Rock of Kuthian and speak your name to open the Vault of Souls"—still remains unfulfilled.

See Angela the herbalist *and* werecats.

"Song of Gerand"
See Gerand.

Sorcery
In contrast to magic, Dragon Rider Oromis has defined sorcery as "a dark and unseemly art" whereby a sorcerer seeks to control supernatural beings to do as he or she commands. A magician desiring to be a sorcerer must spend at least three years of study to learn how to summon spirits and control them. It is a dangerous business, as trapped spirits spend every moment seeking to escape their captivity and take vengeance on their mortal captors. A sorcerer so possessed becomes a Shade.

See Durza *and* magic.

Southern Isles
Off the southwestern coast of Alagaësia lies a cluster of five islands presumed to have been claimed by the Empire: Beirland, Illium, Parlim, Nía, and Uden. Beirland is the largest island in the chain, and the only populated one. It is said that magical phenomena have occurred in the area near Eoam, the island's coastal village. Beirland's notable feature is the Floating Crystal of Eoam, a rare example of what the Dragon Rider Oromis calls wild magic.

Spine, The
The second-largest mountain range in Alagaësia, the Spine covers the entire length of the continent's western coast. Humans have lived here ever since the first settlers arrived in 7203 AC. Villages include Carvahall and Therinsford.

Landmarks range from Edur Carthungavë, also known as Rathbar's Spur, which marks the Spine's southernmost tip, and Igualda Falls, a waterfall at the northern end of Palancar Valley. Measuring over half a mile from top to bottom, the falls are known to have claimed several careless wanderers, including Ismira, wife of Sloan of Carvahall. The unforgiving nature of the region is illustrated by reports of those who venture into the mountains and never return. Even Galbatorix's forces are not immune—a story is told that half his army simply disappeared amid the mountains of the Spine.

Many historic events have happened in the range, beginning with the establishment of those first human settlements. The Spine is where Jarnunvösk, Galbatorix's first dragon, was killed, the tragedy that led to Galbatorix's madness and quest for power. It is where Eragon discovered the dragon egg that made him the first new Dragon Rider in more than a century and a leader in the fight against the Empire.

SPIRITS

Sentient beings composed of pure energy. They can communicate with physical beings and assume many guises and usually induce a rapturous sense of communion in mortals. Eragon himself had an encounter with a spirit that filled him with joy and transcendent happiness—until he realized the supernatural creature was taking over his consciousness. Since spirits are completely unpredictable, it is dangerous for those on the mortal plane to even converse with them.

See Durza *and* Shade.

Star Rose

See Isidar Mithrim.

Star Sapphire
See Isidar Mithrim.

Stone of Broken Eggs
A monolithic tower of basalt north of Ellesméra that rises a hundred feet above the forest and was an ancient habitation of dragons. Towers at the top have black "caves" clawed out of the basalt by the talons of ancient dragons, their floors littered with the remains of their kills. It is a notorious place from the ancient war against dragons and elves. It was here that elves tracked some dragons and killed them in their sleep, tore their nests to pieces, and used magic to shatter the eggs. *That day it rained blood in the forest below,* Saphira told Eragon. *No dragon has lived here since.*
See Du Fyrn Skulblaka.

STRONGHAMMER

See RORAN.

SURDA

This free kingdom of humans, formed in defiance of the Empire, lies on the southern edge of Alagaësia and is today ruled by King Orrin of the House of Langfeld, whose royal lineage reaches back to King Palancar.

Galbatorix is now known to have allowed the secession of Surda, as he was biding his time to strike back. Even Galbatorix's knowledge of Surda's secret alliance with the Varden did not become known until after the Battle in Farthen Dûr. Surda has since taken a leading role in the battle against Galbatorix, with King Orrin dedicated to preserving the Varden alliance and also providing safe haven for refugees and those opposing the Empire.

See LARKIN.

SVARVOK

An Urgal god.

"SWEET AETHRID O' DAUTH"

A popular ballad, of which many versions exist.

TÁBOR, LORD MARCUS

See DRAS-LEONA.

TÁMERLEIN

The sword of the Dragon Rider Arva, which he passed to his sister, Naudra, just before his death. Naudra wielded Támerlein while valiantly fighting by Arva's side during his final day. Támerlein passed into the possession of Lord Fiolr, of the elven House Valtharos, who offered to lend the sword to Eragon.

See ARVA, DRAGON RIDER SWORDS, FIOLR, *and* NAUDRA.

TARMUNORA

The elf queen who signed the original pact with the dragons.

Tarnag

This dwarf surface city is connected to other dwarven cities by a network of tunnels carved throughout the Beor Mountains. Tarnag has been home to three clans: Az Sweldn rak Anhûin, Quan, and Ragni Hefthyn. Despite its thick ramparts, Tarnag fell to Galbatorix's attacks during his war against the Dragon Riders, which led the dwarves to abandon this and other surface cities. After Morzan's death, the dwarves returned to their fabled city.

Dwarven engineering built Tarnag by cutting away terraces of stone upon the mountain, constructing tier upon tier of multicolored stones and interlocking buildings, forming a pyramidal shape topped by a gigantic dome glistening like polished moonstone—Celbedeil, greatest temple of the dwarf nation and home of the Quan clan, whose members serve as messengers to the gods. The buildings themselves are elegantly designed, often decorated with carvings of animals and other figures. At night, the city is illuminated by the multicolored lights of the famous flameless lantern. Eragon visited this city on his way to Ellesméra after the Battle of Farthen Dûr.

See Celbedeil.

Tarok

The third-ranking commander of Galbatorix's Urgal army. Tarok served under Durza and Gashz and oversaw the Urgals during the Battle of Farthen Dûr. After the Empire's defeat at Farthen Dûr, Tarok was missing in action and is presumed dead.

Tarrant

See Ceunon.

Tathal

The traitorous resident of Aberon, Surda's capital city, whose murder plot against a fellow Surdan was telepathically overheard by Eragon, who ensured that Tathal was stopped before he committed his crime.

Tears of Anhûin

See Anhûin.

Teirm

The Empire's largest port city, on the west coast of Alagaësia at the mouth of the Toark River and surrounded by the Spine. Unlike such disorganized and sprawling cities as Dras-Leona, Teirm is one of the best-planned cities in Alagaësia.

Legend holds that Teirm was the landing place for several waves of immigration, from elves to human colonists (although the latter's ships could not make landfall). Although Teirm is the heart of commerce and trade for the Empire, war regularly disrupts business. Espionage and sabotage against the Empire often occur here, as was the case with Jeod, the prosperous Teirm merchant who secretly operated as an agent of the Varden.

The strategic port city has historically known threat—it was once almost razed by pirates. The city has since gone to extraordinary lengths to build up its defenses, including a hundred-foot-tall, thirty-foot-thick stone wall that surrounds the city and is lined with sentries, archers, and patrolling soldiers. Within its walls, the tiered layout of buildings with flat roofs allows archers to be stationed for another line of offense. Teirm's signature architectural landmark is a citadel built of giant stones with a tower that serves as the city's lighthouse. However, many of Teirm's cobblestone streets are choked with weeds, and housing in the poorer districts is ramshackle at best. The wealthy and powerful live on the West Side, a district that has been home to Jeod and the shop of Angela the herbalist. Both Eragon and Roran have passed through Teirm. Eragon stopped here with Brom and met Jeod Longshanks and Angela the herbalist for the first time. Roran stole a ship from Teirm to carry the people of Carvahall down the coast. It was here that he learned Eragon is a Dragon Rider.

See Dras-Leona.

Tenga

Ingvar's son and a hermit dweller within a tower of the Edur Ithindra ruins, which Tenga has claimed as a library for his scrolls and books. Proficient in the ancient language and skilled in magic, Tenga mentored Angela the herbalist. Tenga has dedicated his solitary existence to divining the secrets of the elemental forces of trees, other plants, fire, and light. Eragon met Tenga on his way back to the Varden after killing the Ra'zac in Helgrind. He helped the old man garden, noted his wordless use of magic, marveled at his library, shared a lunch with him, and saw some wooden animal statues—but after some odd conversation, Eragon concluded that Tenga was mad and slipped away quietly. Later, when Eragon asked Angela about Tenga, she noted that Tenga is deranged but brilliant, although the werecat Solembum has derisively said of the hermit, "He is a man who kicks at cats."

See Angela the herbalist.

Thanebrand the Ring Giver

See Broddring Kingdom.

THARDÛR

Mountain where the Ingeitum clan built Bregan Hold.

THERINSFORD

A small village of the Empire in the heart of Palancar Valley notorious for its poor planning. Surrounded by rich farmland, Therinsford is accessible by a bridge across the Anora River. Just south of Therinsford is the lonely mountain of Utgard with its watchtower Edoc'sil. Roran left his father's farm to become a miller's apprentice in Therinsford and was there when the Ra'zac killed Garrow. Eragon and Brom bought horses just outside of Therinsford as they left Palancar Valley in search of the Ra'zac.

See BRODDRING KINGDOM.

THIRTEEN FORSWORN

See FORSWORN.

THORDRIS

Dwarf chief of the Dûrgrimst Nagra.
See DWARF CLANS *IN THE APPENDIX*.

THORGERD ONE-EYE

The husband of Himinglada, the father of Hvedra.

THORN

The youngest dragon in Alagaësia, hatched from one of the three dragon eggs to survive the Fall of the Riders. Thorn had rested within his egg for a century but hatched for Murtagh soon after the Battle of Farthen Dûr. Galbatorix then forced both Rider and dragon to swear (in the ancient language) their loyalty to him. Knowing their true names, Galbatorix has the power to enslave them. With his blood-red scales, snow-white spikes, and muscular body, this dragon strikes fear into those who face him

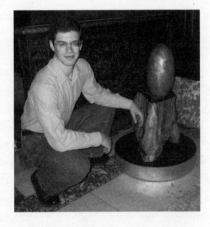

and Murtagh. During the Battle of the Burning Plains, Eragon wounded Thorn, but Murtagh mysteriously healed him in just a few seconds and proceeded to capture Eragon.

Arya explained to Eragon that Galbatorix probably used magic to accelerate Thorn's physical growth, leaving him with the mind of a youngling but the body of an adult. By the second encounter between Eragon-Saphira and Murtagh-Thorn, when the latter sought out the former at the Varden camp, Thorn had grown rapidly again. In that fight—with wounds and healing magic on both sides—Eragon and Saphira prevailed with the help of the elven guard. Murtagh and Thorn retreated to Galbatorix's army, having failed to achieve their goal of capturing Eragon and Saphira.

At Gil'ead, when Oromis and Glaedr emerge from Ellesméra, Thorn and Murtagh defeat them, slaying Oromis and also Glaedr's physical body, though his Eldunarí lives on.

See Murtagh.

Thorv

One of the guards of the dwarf clan chief Ûndin.

Thrand

A renegade dwarf warrior of Dûrgrimst Ingeitum, Thrand achieved renown as Eragon's lead guard and captain of a small band of dwarves during Eragon's visits to Farthen Dûr. The one attack upon Eragon by dwarf assassins was repelled by Thrand and his guards with minimal losses.

Thrifk

The father of Orik.

Thun

A small town in Surda, formerly ruled by Martland Redbeard.

Tialdarí Hall

Queen Islanzadí's family hall in Ellesméra. It was here that she put the writing that Eragon shared with the elven nation during the Agaetí Blödhren.

Togira Ikonoka

See Oromis and Glaedr.

Torkenbrand
See slavery.

Tornac
Murtagh's friend, servant, and fencing instructor in Uru'baen. Tornac was a skilled swordsman but was slain while fleeing Uru'baen with Murtagh. Murtagh named his horse Tornac in honor of the man who taught him how to fight.

Torson
The first mate to Clovis the fisherman.

Tosk
Author of the eponymous book that lays out the rules for worshipers of the dark forces at the mystical site of Helgrind.

Travels of Gnaevaldrskald
See Gnaevaldrskald.

Trevor

A soldier who had once served in Galbatorix's army but, once settled in the village of Daret, was chosen by villagers there to defend their town against Urgals and other potential invaders.

Trial of the Long Knives

A brutal and unforgiving test of leadership in which opponents take turns cutting their own forearms, the bloodletting continuing until one relents. By this ancient test, Nasuada was challenged for leadership by the warlord Fadawar. As drums pounded, each took turns making knife cuts. Fadawar had made eight bloody slices, but Nasuada bested him with two cuts in a row. The warlord attempted a ninth cut but was forced to say, "I submit." According to the rules, Nasuada's wounds may not be healed with magic; otherwise her victory is forfeit.

See Fadawar.

Trianna

A sorceress in Du Vrangr Gata with the Varden. With the death of the Twins, she became leader of that group of spellcasters. She has flirted with Eragon, who seemed amenable to her advances until Saphira intervened and called her a "slattern." She wears a gold bracelet shaped like a serpent, which she calls Lorga, her "familiar and protector." Nasuada doesn't fully trust her, but she does command Trianna to use her magic to produce lace so that the Varden can sell it to fund their war against the Empire—and Trianna fulfills that command. Trianna also helped protect Nasuada from the assassin Drail. Later, she used her magic, along with Angela the herbalist's balms, to heal the lashes Roran had received for insubordination, which allowed him to lead a Varden coalition on the city of Feinster.

See RORAN.

TRÍHGA

One of the guards for the dwarf clan chief Ûndin.

TRONJHEIM

The capital of the dwarf nation and the largest city within the heart of Farthen Dûr, the hollowed crater within the Beor Mountains. Crafted from marble many millennia ago, this is one of the wonders of the world—the "city-mountain," as Eragon has called it—and big enough to house the entire nation. The city rises a mile high and is built with levels for housing the population. It is accessed via tunnels leading to gigantic wooden gates blocking the city's entrance, and its peak is open to the sky. The capital has been called the City of Eternal Twilight, as the city-mountain receives sunlight for a single hour in summertime. Because of the perpetual shadow, the dwarves have lit the city with a virtually endless supply of flameless lanterns. Tronjheim is not self-sustaining and relies on a trade in food and supplies from nearby dwarf settlements.

The dwarves allowed the Varden to shelter within Farthen Dûr, a risky decision and one that threatened the dwarven people when the Empire's Urgal army invaded Farthen Dûr. Although many dwarf and Varden soldiers died, they won the battle and the city was spared from destruction. The Varden population has since relocated to Surda, with the dwarves traversing back and forth between Farthen Dûr and the Varden's camp.

See SURDA *AND* VOL TURIN.

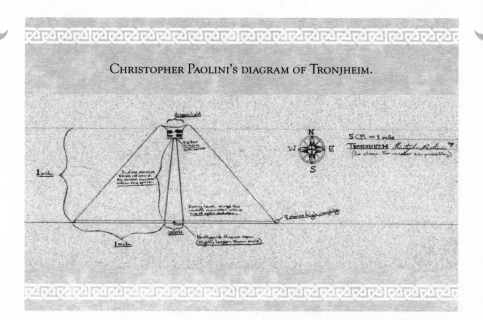

CHRISTOPHER PAOLINI'S DIAGRAM OF TRONJHEIM.

TRUE NAME

In addition to a common name, everything (objects, plants, animals, people) has a true name in the ancient language. Knowing another's true name gives one power over that individual or object. Eragon used his knowledge of Sloan's true name to compel him to go to Ellesméra, and Galbatorix used Murtagh's true name to enslave him. Most people do not know their own true name.

See ANCIENT LANGUAGE.

TUATHA DU OROTHRIM

Translates as "tempering the fool's wisdom," a level in a Dragon Rider's training.

TÚNIVOR'S NECTAR

A powerful healing potion invented by the elf alchemist of the same name. The main ingredient is the glossy black cap of the poisonous Fricai Andlát mushroom (the only palatable part), found within Du Weldenvarden and Farthen Dûr. Túnivor's Nectar is used to cure many wounds and ailments and is the only known antidote to the Skilna Bragh, a poison favored by the Empire's assassins.

TWINS

A pair of identical twin magicians who ostensibly served the Varden government but who were secret agents of Galbatorix. They joined Du Vrangr Gata when the nation needed spellcasters, but their manipulative and arrogant nature made them unpopular. However, their command of the ancient language and their ability to fuse their telepathic powers made them deadly spellcasters and a vital asset. It was the Twins who judged Eragon's ability to wield the forces of magic and grudgingly told Ajihad he was "competent in all magic."

When their bloodied robes were found after the Battle of Farthen Dûr, the Twins were presumed dead. The Twins' treason was revealed, however, when they reappeared on the side of the Empire during the Battle of the Burning Plains. They were slain on the battlefield by Roran, who caught the traitors from behind, killing each with mighty blows of his hammer.

See Roran.

Uden

See Southern Isles.

Ulhart

Right-hand man to Martland Redbeard.

Ulric

A dockworker in Narda.

UMÉRTH
See COUNCIL OF ELDERS.

UMHODAN
The legendary elf from *The Lay of Umhodan*.

UNDBITR
See DRAGON RIDER SWORDS.

ÛNDIN
Current clan chief of Ragni Hefthyn and son of Derûnd.
See DWARF CLANS *IN THE APPENDIX.*

UNKNOWN SOLDIER
The mysterious soldier in Galbatorix's army who left a white rose for Arya during her imprisonment in Gil'ead, the only act of kindness and mercy she received before being rescued by Eragon, Saphira, and Murtagh.

UNULUKUNA
Creator god of the wandering tribes. Also known as the Old One.

Urgals

The race that calls itself the Urgralgra, the Urgals are considered the continent's most brutal and violent race—and the most hated. Urgals physically resemble gigantic muscular humans, but they bear long, twisted horns and have thick grayish skin and yellow eyes. Adding to their fearsome renown is a smell that other races often find offensive. Urgals usually wear a simple loincloth and are rarely seen without swords, axes, and rough-hewn shields. The elite of the Urgals are the outsized Kull.

Urgal society is more complex than their violent and brutish appearance and reputation suggest. They are known to engage in shamanistic practices. An elaborate courtship ritual is the creation of a hearth rug, which takes five years to complete; during that time a couple has time to evaluate their compatibility and affection for each other. It is said that Urgal marriages are as caring and loving as any among the other races of Alagaësia.

The Shade Durza used his magic to gain power over the warlike and independent Urgals, forming an Urgal army to fight for Galbatorix. Durza led the Urgal forces to the gates of Farthen Dûr, where the Empire sought to strike a decisive blow against the Varden. The Empire's defeat, and Durza's death, freed the Urgals from the Shade's enchantments. The Bolvek tribe of Urgals, whose leader is the Kull Nar Garzhvog, allied themselves with the Varden before the Battle of the Burning Plains.

See Battle of the Burning Plains *and* Bolvek.

URGAL HORNS ARE SIMILAR TO THOSE OF THE FELDÛNOST, WHICH RESEMBLE THOSE OF BIGHORN SHEEP.

URÛ'BAEN

Currently the capital of Galbatorix's Empire. The city has a rich history, beginning as the elven city known as Ilirea, which was destroyed and abandoned during the elves' ancient war against the dragons. The land was later claimed by the first human settlers, who established their own capital there. The city has become a darker place under Galbatorix, who has expanded what is now called the dark citadel. At the heart of the capital is Castle Ilirea, home to a long lineage of rulers and now where Galbatorix rules and holds the last remaining dragon egg.

See Ilirea.

URÛR

A dwarven god, master of the air and heavens. Urûr and his brother, Morgothal, god of fire, are so devoted to each other that they can't exist independently. According to dwarven myth, these brother gods joined forces and brought dragons into the world.

URZHAD

The mighty cave bear, one of the five animals unique to the Beor Mountains. Despite their gigantic size, Urzhadn can move with amazing speed. Called Beor in the ancient language.

THE URZHAD IS BASED ON THE EXTINCT GIANT CAVE BEAR. THE MOST SIMILAR CREATURE ALIVE TODAY IS THE KODIAK BEAR OF ALASKA.

USHNARK THE MIGHTY
SEE GALBATORIX.

UTGARD MOUNTAIN

A lonely mountain in the Spine at the southern end of Palancar Valley, past Therinsford. After King Palancar was overthrown, the watchtower Edoc'sil ("Unconquerable") was built here by the elves as a strategic point to allow Dragon Riders to keep watch over the humans and their descendants. It was on Utgard Mountain that a wounded Vrael, leader of the last of the Dragon Riders, fled to recover from injuries suffered in battle with Galbatorix and where Galbatorix found and beheaded him. The watchtower remains but is now known as Ristvak'baen ("Place of Sorrow").

UTHAR

A seasoned sailor of Teirm who accompanied the Carvahall villagers on the voyage to Surda. As captain of the pirated *Dragon Wing*, he escaped Galbatorix's forces by sailing through the maelstrom of the Boar's Eye, earning him renown as one of the greatest mariners of all time.

SEE BOAR'S EYE.

VACHER

A human philosopher whose vacuum theory was disproved by both King Orrin and Ládin, the elf philosopher.

VÁNDIŁ

One of the greatest elf spellweavers.

VANIR

A young elf of the House of Haldthin who easily defeated Eragon in sparring sessions of swordsmanship during Eragon's training in Ellesméra. Vanir was openly contemptuous of Eragon, often accusing him of being an unfit Rider, but finally gave due respect after Eragon was blessed during the Agaetí Blödhren.

Eragon easily defeated Vanir in their last duel, giving the haughty elf a broken arm.

SEE LAY OF UMHODAN, THE.

VARAUG

The Shade conjured by Empire magicians during the Siege of Feinster, and ultimately slain by Arya.

SEE SIEGE OF FEINSTER.

VARDEN, THE

After Galbatorix's declaration of victory in his power struggle with the Dragon Riders, a band of humans, led by the Dragon Rider Brom, formed the resistance movement known as the Varden ("Wanderers" in the ancient language). Its succession of leaders, from Deynon to Ajihad to Nasuada, built the rebel group into a formidable opposition capable of waging war against the Empire. Along the way, the Varden have forged alliances with dwarves, elves, and the human state of Surda. For a long time the Varden took refuge in the dwarves' realm of Farthen Dûr. After the Battle of Farthen Dûr, and under Nasuada's leadership, the Varden relocated to Surda. The Varden's recent victories over the Empire have inspired confidence within the remainder of Alagaësia's neutral factions. The elusive race of werecats, as well as a revered clan of Urgal fighters, have since joined in the fight against Galbatorix.

VARDRÛN

The mother of Himinglada and grandmother of Hvedra.

VAULT OF SOULS, THE

Unknown place mentioned by the werecat Solembum when Angela the herbalist read Eragon's fortune. Solembum's advice: "When all seems lost and your power is insufficient, go to the Rock of Kuthian and speak your name to open the Vault of Souls."

VERMÛND

The dwarf chief of the Az Sweldn rak Anhûin clan who was implicated in the attempted assassination of Eragon. During the clanmeet that elected Orik the new monarch, Vermûnd was sentenced to the ultimate dwarven punishment— banishment. In dwarven culture, this means not only physical exile, but treating the offender as if they had never existed.

See RIMMAR.

VERVADA

See IORMÚNGR.

VESTARÍ

Legendary elf from *The Lay of Vestarí the Mariner*.

VOL TURIN

Also known as the Endless Staircase, Vol Turin is the spiral staircase in the inner walls of Tronjheim that connects each level of the gigantic pyramidal city.

During an emergency, dwarves communicate along the staircase with lanterns. A smooth trough was subsequently built alongside the spiraling staircase to allow one to slide from the top to the bottom in under ten minutes. But visitors beware—the speed trough was built for dwarves and is a very risky ride for those with bigger bodies.

See Tronjheim.

Volund

The war hammer forged by Korgan Longbeard, first king of the dwarves, which has been wielded by dwarf kings and queens.

Vrael

Leader of the Dragon Riders and the last to fall to Galbatorix's bloody purge of the Riders. An ancient Rider, Vrael not only tried to keep the remaining dragons from the clutches of Galbatorix but also came close to ending Galbatorix's mad dreams forever. The two were in battle before the gates of the Dragon Rider's capital city of Doru Araeba when Vrael seemingly defeated Galbatorix and had raised his sword to end it all, but he hesitated—and in that moment's pause, the cause of freedom was undone. Galbatorix took the moment to recover and strike back, wounding Vrael.

Thereafter, Vrael became the hunted. He fled to Utgard Mountain, where Galbatorix found him and ended their fight with a stroke of his sword, beheading the brave Dragon Rider. Next he overthrew Angrenost, the reigning king, and declared himself king of Alagaësia.

See Dragon Riders *and* Utgard Mountain.

VROENGARD

An island off Alagaësia's northwestern shore and home to Doru Araeba, capital city of the Dragon Riders. Vroengard is now abandoned, a grim reminder of Galbatorix's defeat of the mighty Dragon Riders.

WAKING DREAMS

Elves do not sleep and dream like mortals but instead experience "waking dreams," a trancelike state that produces vivid, hallucinatory visions. After the Ayaetí Blödhren, Eragon, too, rests and restores with waking dreams.

WANDERING TRIBES

In 7209 AC, only three years after humans were accepted into the pact between dragons and elves, a ship arrived in Alagaësia bearing dark-skinned humans. They are the ancestors of today's nomadic tribes, as well as the artisans who can be found in the cities of Aroughs, Dauth, and Aberon. The latter's skill and renown as craftsmen and jewelers have made them a wealthy people.

WARLORD

The title among the tribal peoples given to the one who leads a coalition of at least two tribes.

WAVERUNNER

A Nardan ship.

WELMAR

A Varden warrior who served under Martland Redbeard.

WERECATS

The werecats are an ancient race of which little is known other than that they may have magical powers, live longer than humans, and know more than they tell. They are shapeshifters who can take the form of a large cat or a small person. In addition to their innate power to foretell the future, these cunning creatures are proficient combatants, capable of fighting in either cat or humanoid form. Most werecats choose to keep to themselves, living and traveling alone in obscurity, though a few have been known to form companionships alongside respected members of outside races.

Most members of the mysterious race disappeared shortly after the Fall of the Riders and the race slowly faded into legends. The werecats recently resurfaced after nearly a century in hiding to form an alliance with the Varden in the war against the Empire. Though their numbers are few, their prowess in battle and their leader's ability to command the feral cats of Alagaësia will prove to be crucial in securing the Varden's position in the war.

The werecats have mostly chosen to remain neutral throughout Alagaësia's past conflicts. However, during exceptional times when the werecats have felt wronged or threatened, the race has come together to elect a leader to take them into battle. The leader, known as the king of werecats, is responsible for speaking for his race during the war.

AT THE SUGGESTION OF HIS SISTER, ANGELA, PAOLINI DERIVED PHYSICAL DESCRIPTIONS OF WERECATS FROM THE CARACAL, A SPECIES OF MEDIUM-SIZED CAT NATIVE TO AFRICA AND WESTERN ASIA.

WERELIGHT

A small ball of light that is magically conjured. Werelights can be used to light one's way or be rooted in place to illuminate a specific area.

See WILD MAGIC.

WILD MAGIC

The term Oromis has used to describe how magic can exist "on its own, independent of any spell." Such magical phenomena include the Dream Well in Mani's Caves in the Beor Mountains, the werelights that can be seen in the bogs near Aroughs, and the Floating Crystal of Eoam. (Such wild magic is by its nature unpredictable and dangerous.)

Wyglif

A Carvahall resident who died while defending his village from the Empire.

Wyrdfell

See Forsworn.

ΥARBOG

A member of the Bolvek tribe, which allied with the Varden in exchange for a promise of land. During one raid, Yarbog became disgruntled with Roran's leadership and challenged him to a fight to determine who could best lead the raiding parties. Yarbog was defeated and forced to submit to Roran's leadership. The incident illustrated the Varden leader Nasuada's fears that their alliance with the Urgals was beginning to come apart, though Roran's victory helped to smooth it.

SEE RORAN *AND* URGALS.

ΥAWË

An elven rune from the Liduen Kvaedhí, the elf script that indicates devotion to the elven race. Arya had the symbol tattooed on her shoulder. This mystic symbol also adorns the ring Aren, which was given to Brom, and later Eragon, by the elves.

YAZUAC

A small Empire town on the banks of the Ninor River, reportedly filled with enemies of the Empire and their sympathizers. Yazuac was destroyed by Urgal forces presumably acting on Galbatorix's orders. Eragon passed through this town with Brom, and it was here that he first uttered "Brisingr" and used magic for the first time.

YAZUAC IS A NEAR ANAGRAM FOR THE *YAKUZA*, THE JAPANESE MAFIA.

Z

ZAR'ROC

See DRAGON RIDER SWORDS.

Appendix

Dragons and Riders

Although little is generally known about individual dragons, there are extant accounts chronicling the exploits of certain dragons and Riders. The following have been mentioned.

Dragons

Eridor
Fundor
Lenora
Miremel
Opheila

Riders

Beroan
Briam
Galzra
Gretiem
Hírador
Ingothold
Jura
Ohen the Strong
Roslarb

Dwarf Clans

Dûrgrimst Az Sweldn rak Anhûin: Nearly destroyed by Galbatorix and the Forsworn, this clan developed a hatred of dragons and Riders. They declared themselves sworn blood enemies of Eragon and Saphira and, in an incident that brought shame on their clan, violated the Law of Hospitality by attempting to kill Eragon, who was guest of a dwarf clanmeet.

Dûrgrimst Ebardac: The clan devoted to scholarly research.

Dûrgrimst Fanghur: Clan named after the dragonlike creature that dwells in the Beor Mountains.

Dûrgrimst Feldûnost: Clan named after the mountain goat indigenous to the Beor Mountains. Although other clans are named after animals native to the Beor Mountains, the Feldûnost is considered so important to dwarven survival in the Beors that this clan is among the most respected.

Dûrgrimst Gedthrall: A clan of skilled artisans, Gedthrall was entrusted with the monumental task of repairing the shattered Isidar Mithrim.

Dûrgrimst Ingeitum: Considered one of the most powerful of the clans, in the recent era they have produced two kings, Hrothgar and Orik, who, in series, have ruled for a hundred years.

Dûrgrimst Knurlcarathn: The stoneworkers' clan. Their skills at building and tunneling have no equal in Alagaësia and have made them a vital resource for all the clans.

Dûrgrimst Ledwonnû: The name translates as "Kílf's necklace."

Dûrgrimst Nagra: Clan named after the mighty boars of the Beor Mountains, beasts hunted by only the bravest of dwarves and whose prized meat is served at feasts honoring those of great courage.

Dûrgrimst Quan: The custodians of the dwarves' religion, considered the servants and messengers of the gods. As such, this clan wields enormous influence among all of the race. The sacred works of the dwarven people are written by the Quan in the secret rune alphabet of the Mahlvikn.

Dûrgrimst Ragni Hefthyn: This clan, known as the "River Guard," is based in the surface city of Tarnag. Although the Quan clan is also based here, they are small in number, and the Ragni Hefthyn are considered to be in control of Tarnag.

Dûrgrimst Urzhadn: The cave bear clan.

Dûrgrimst Vrenshrrgn: A powerful, warlike clan. Also known as "War Wolves."

ELF FAMILIES

House of Dröttning

House of Haldthin

House of Miolandra

House of Orthindr

House of Rílvenar

House of Thrándurin (the extinct house of the Dragon Rider Oromis)

House of Valtharos

MOUNTAINS

Beor Mountains: The mighty range in the southern half of the continent.

Edur Carthungavë: Considered the "tailbone" of the Spine; also called Rathbur's Spur.

Ethrundr: South of Ellesméra.

Fionula: South of Ellesméra.

Griminsmal: South of Ellesméra.

Helgrind: Three peaks—Fell Angvara, Gorm, and Ilda.

Iron Cliffs: The rise before the southernmost tip of the Spine.

Merogoven: South of Ellesméra.

Narnmor Mountain: Near Igualda Falls in the Spine.

Residents of Carvahall

The following residents of Carvahall are mentioned briefly or in passing:

Albem
Bardrick
Bartram
Brenna
Calitha
Darmmen
Ethlbert
Farold
Garner
Ged
Hale
Hida
Ivor
Kelby
Kiselt
Knute
Melkolf
Nesbit
Nolla
Orval
Parr
Ridley
Sardson
Southwell
Svart
Tara
Thane
Wayland

Rivers and Lakes

Anora River: Runs along the northern reaches of the Spine, near the villages of Carvahall and Therinsford.

Ardwen: A lake in the great forest of Du Weldenvarden.

Az Ragni: Runs from the lake near Tarnag in the Beor Mountains to the dwarven outpost of Hedarth.

Beartooth River: Flows out of a valley in the Beor Mountains.

Edda River: Flows from Eldor Lake.

Eldor: A lake on the eastern edge of Du Weldenvarden.

Fernoth-mérna: A lake in the Odred Valley whose northern end reaches the Ragni Darmn river, which flows through the valley until it meets up with the Az Ragni.

Fläm: A lake at the central-eastern edge of the Spine.

Gaena River: Meanders from Lake Ardwen in an easterly path out of the great forest to Eldor Lake.

Isenstar: A lake on the westerly tip of Du Weldenvarden.

Jiet River: Travels from Leona Lake south to where the land meets the sea.

Kóstha-mérna: A lake just outside Farthen Dûr.

Leona: A lake near Dras-Leona.

Nalsvrid-mérna: A lake in the Beor Mountains.

Ninor River: Runs near the Spine and the city of Daret and meets Lake Isenstar.

Nost Creek: Lies within Palancar Valley.

Ragni Darmn: Flows north from Fernoth-mérna until it joins the Az Ragni near the foothills of Moldûn the Proud.

Ramr River: Runs south from Isenstar Lake and past Galbatorix's stronghold of Urû'baen.

Röna: A lake in the depths of Du Weldenvarden, with Nädindel the nearest city.

Toark River: Runs from the western sea and travels through the Spine to Leona Lake.

Tüdosten: A lake near Silverwood Forest.

Woardark Lake: A tiny body of water in the Spine intersected by the Toark River.